## "This is not a game. I don't play games."

His warning was quiet but his hand grasped her wrist, forcing her to drop the telephone receiver.

"Don't you?" Samantha's brown eyes shimmered with defiance. Temper threw caution to the winds. "You've been playing games with me all along—first letting me believe you were Owen Bradley, then lying—" She bit her lip, realizing she had virtually admitted that she knew he wasn't who he pretended to be.

The narrowing of his gaze indicated he had guessed what she'd been about to say. Her heart skipped several beats, but she had gone too far to turn back now.

"I don't know who you are," she said flatly, "but you aren't Chris Andrews!"

## JANET DAILEY AMERICANA

# Janet Dailey
## Americana

# BEWARE
# OF THE STRANGER

## Harlequin Books

TORONTO • NEW YORK • LONDON
AMSTERDAM • PARIS • SYDNEY • HAMBURG
STOCKHOLM • ATHENS • TOKYO • MILAN
MADRID • WARSAW • BUDAPEST • AUCKLAND

The state flower depicted on the cover of this book is rose.

Janet Dailey Americana edition published September 1987
Second printing August 1988
Third printing August 1989
Fourth printing August 1990
Fifth printing October 1991
Sixth printing May 1992

ISBN 0-373-89882-7

Harlequin Presents edition published October 1976
Second printing April 1981

Original hardcover edition published in 1978
by Mills & Boon Limited

BEWARE OF THE STRANGER

# CHAPTER ONE

SAMANTHA'S FINGERS punched relentlessly at the typewriter keys. A furrow of concentration formed between her dark eyebrows and the line of her mouth was grim with determination. Regardless of her efforts, she couldn't achieve any speed with the manual typewriter. She might as well have been pecking the keys with one finger. Her little finger missed the "a" in "Yale" and the typed word became "Yle."

Sighing impatiently, Samantha reached for the eraser, nearly worn out from frequent use. The image of the sleek electric typewriter at home flitted wistfully through her mind. If only she could bring it to work, she thought, and immediately shelved the idea. An expensive model like that would raise too many eyebrows and too many questions.

The eraser gouged a hole in the paper, completely obliterating the error. "Damn!" Samantha muttered in exasperation, and ripped the sheet from the carriage.

"Problems?" The question was loaded with good-natured ribbing.

Samantha shot the dark-haired girl a quelling look. "None that a little manual dexterity wouldn't cure.

Why don't you lend me some of yours, Beth? You can afford it."

The snappish reply carried a trace of envy. There wasn't a machine in the place that Beth couldn't operate with lightning speed and efficiency. It didn't matter whether it was a manual or an electric typewriter, a copy machine or the teletype in the adjoining news wire room.

"Poor Sammi," Beth laughed. "Why don't you try the one-finger, hunt and peck method? Mr. Lindsey has used it for years." Referring to their mutual boss and the owner-editor of the newspaper.

"This is one reporter who's going to be a speedy typist—even if I have a mental breakdown first," Samantha grimaced, but her sense of humor had returned, however wryly.

"What are you working on?" Beth ignored the comment except for a faintly sympathetic smile that touched her lips. "I'm not busy. Maybe I can type it for you?"

"No, thanks." Samantha shook her head firmly, thick, luxurious seal-brown hair rippling about her shoulders. "It's the Around and About column. It's so dull you'd fall asleep before you were half-done. I wish Har—Mr. Lindsey would let me spice it up a bit." She quickly corrected her near reference to their boss by his first name.

Beth wrinkled her nose. "How could you ever spice up that boring column? 'Mrs. Carmichael's daughter Susan was home for the weekend.' 'Mr. and Mrs. Donald Bradshaw entertained guests from out of state.'" She irreverently mimicked the type of copy that appeared in the column.

"It would be easy," Samantha asserted, "if I were allowed to do a little snooping. Take this item about Frank Howard, our esteemed attorney and Yale graduate, who had one of his former classmates spend the weekend. It just happens that this former classmate applied for the position of District School Superintendent and Frank Howard just happens to be chairman of the school board. Now if that doesn't smack of political maneuvering and collusion, nothing does."

"Really?" Beth breathed, her eyes widening at that piece of gossip. "But no one's been offered the position yet?"

"Not yet," Samantha agreed dryly. "But I doubt if anyone else will get it other than our chairman's friend and fellow alumnus."

"Does the boss know?"

"Yes." She inserted a new sheet of paper into the typewriter and turned her disgruntled expression to her notes. "And he reminded me that he doesn't print that type of column."

Harry Lindsey had said a bit more than that. Samantha had listened to his twenty-minute lecture concerning the diplomacy needed to operate a small-town newspaper. He had pointed out that any of the innocent items in the column could be turned, through conjecture and supposition, into juicy gossip, a fact Samantha was well aware of.

He had also forcefully pointed out that these same

people who liked to see their names in print in the innocent column were generally business people in the community. The same business people he relied on to run advertisements in his newspapers and provide him with an income to keep the newspaper going. And a good editor didn't offend his clients just to sell copies unless there was ample justification. A little political back-scratching did not fall into that category unless there was fraud or criminal intention involved.

It was a statement Samantha couldn't throw stones at for fear one of them would boomerang. Her father did plenty of back-scratching. It was his considerable influence that had obtained her this job with Harry Lindsey for the summer. She had wanted to learn the basics of newspaper reporting, and what better place to do it than on the staff of a small-town newspaper? With this experience and a diploma in journalism that would be in her hands at the end of her next college year, Samantha was confident that she could get a job with a big publication. Her ambition was to become one of the best investigative reporters around.

But realistically, Samantha sighed, she had to concede the wisdom of Harry's attitude. For the time being, she would simply have to stem the instinctive urge to delve below the surface of a given situation. Her natural curiosity could run free later when she had achieved her ambition.

It wasn't a goal she talked about too much. Few people she knew would understand her desire. Most of her female classmates and even her co-workers on the paper, such as Beth, still considered work of secondary importance. Their first ambition was to find a man, with luck, to marry. There were one or two who were as dedicated as Samantha was to the pursuit of their careers, but each one also planned to have a man to share in her future.

At twenty-two, Samantha had few illusions left about men, at least as far as she was concerned. She didn't hate them or even dislike them. Samantha had simply faced the fact that there never could be "one" man in her life.

It wasn't that she was repulsive to look at—quite the contrary. Her freshly scrubbed, wholesome features were quite pleasing to the eye. There was even a suggestion of sensuality to the curve of her lips. The brown of her eyes, the same richly dark shade as her hair, sparkled often with animation and a zest for life. There was a frankness to their expression that was decidedly fresh and appealing. Her eyes didn't know how to be coy and flirt. Occasionally there was a glimmer of shrewdness in the warm brown depths, an inheritance from her father and a trait that Samantha intended to put to use in her chosen career.

The truth was that she was every man's ideal of a perfect sister. It was a backhanded compliment received so often that it had lost its sting. That could have been overcome with the right man. But Samantha doubted that there was a man alive who could overcome her biggest obstacle.

This summer's charade had pointed that out to her.

Being a new female face in a small town had attracted
a lot of male attention to Samantha. Most of it was
dissolved by her sisterly looks. At a local dance, she
had overheard her date being teased that it must be
like kissing his sister when he took her home. It was
the last time the man had asked her out.

The few, very few, who had remained attentive
would run to the hills the minute they found out she
was Reuben Gentry's daughter, Samantha knew. She
had discovered very early in life that the male ego was
too fragile. Men weren't willing to marry a woman
whose father would overshadow them their entire
lives. Unless they wanted to share in the wealth and
power he commanded, and Samantha wanted no part
of that kind of man. Thanks to the shrewd perception
she had inherited from her father, she usually spotted
that kind the instant she met them and steered clear.

For a while Samantha had thought if she could find
a man as powerful and wealthy as her father, she
wouldn't have to worry about the problem of being
Reuben Gentry's daughter. She had even been en-
gaged to such a man when she was eighteen, but it
had lasted only a month. She had found out two
things. One was that money always wants more
money and her fiancé considered their engagement
more of a business alliance with her father. And sec-
ondly, she didn't love the man.

The broken engagement had also brought an end to
any plans for a man in her life—at least in the singu-
lar. In time she would probably have affairs with men.
She was a red-blooded woman with physical needs,

too. It was even possible that she would fall in love with someone, but it wouldn't last—Samantha knew that. She loathed the terms "spinster" and "old maid." She preferred to think of herself as a confirmed "bachelorette." In these liberated times there was nothing to be ashamed of in not being married.

Reuben Gentry had always silently understood the burden she carried as his daughter. Only once had he said anything about it, and that had been after her engagement was broken and Samantha had explained why she had done it. He had suggested that she might prefer some anonymity, hinting that he wouldn't object if she changed her name.

Samantha had refused outright, declaring, "I'm not ashamed of who I am!"

Her cheeks dimpled slightly as Samantha concealed a smile. Only for this summer had she concealed her identity, wanting to work for the small newspaper without the usual notioriety that followed her. The smile continued to play about the corners of her mouth. Only minutes ago she had been wanting to spice up the column with a bit of gossip. And she was the biggest story in the entire town. Imagine how everyone would be set back on their heels if they found out that the innocuous Samantha Jones was really *the* Samantha Gentry!

"What are you smiling about?" Beth wanted to know.

Samantha let her mouth curve into a full smile. "Just imagining the readers' reactions if I actually printed the truth," she replied, without explaining further her exact meaning.

Beth shrugged, not finding the idea nearly as humorous as Samantha did. She continued flipping through the magazine lying on her desk and stopped turning pages when a particular article caught her interest.

"Here's my horoscope for the month," Beth said aloud and began reading it. "'June will be a calm month with plenty of warmth and laughter. Weekends will mean pleasant jaunts but not too far from home. Your closest friends will be a source of joy.' Nothing about weddings," she sighed. She glanced over the rest of the page. "Here's yours, Sammi. Do you want to hear it?"

"I dont' care," Samantha shrugged. She didn't put any stock in horoscopes. To her they always seemed to be couched in words that could be interpreted any way the reader wanted.

Her lack of enthusiasm didn't deter Beth. "'June will be an uncertain month. Beware of strangers entering your life. They may not be what they represent. Check the facts before trusting your intuition. Travel is not recommended.'"

"Wait until I tell the boss that," Samantha laughed. "I've finally got him to agree to let me do a feature article on that lady celebrating her hundredth birthday in the next town, and now I'll have to tell him I can't do it because my horoscope says travel isn't recommended."

"He'll be furious," Beth agreed seriously.

"Oh, honestly, you don't really believe all that hogwash, do you?" Samantha declared with an incredulous shake of her head. She had been kidding, but Beth seemed to have taken her joke literally.

There was a defensive tilt of Beth's chin. "These forecasts are quite accurate."

"It depends on how you read between the lines," Samantha muttered, a little surprised that someone as efficient and practical as Beth could be superstitious about astrology forecasts. Most of them were turned out as haphazardly as pieces of paper in a fortune cookie.

But she wasn't about to become embroiled in any discussion about the facts or fantasies of astrology. With a dismissive shake of her head, Samantha turned back to the paper in her typewriter and began punching away at the keys. Beth said no more, slightly offended by Samantha's openly skeptical attitude toward something she half, if not completely, believed to be gospel.

When the column was typed, Samantha removed it from the carriage and began double-checking the spelling of the names with her notes. The street door opened and Samantha glanced up automatically. The tall, dark-haired stranger who walked in caught and held her attention.

Although Samantha had been living in the small town less than a month, intuition told her positively that the man was not a local resident. He was dressed casually in a forest green blazer and plaid slacks, nothing flashy nor overly affluent. His easygoing air wouldn't attract attention, yet Samantha couldn't shake the feeling that word would have reached her if there was such a man around. He wasn't the kind anyone ignored.

He walked directly to Beth's desk, which, besides being a reception desk, doubled as the classified advertisement section. Behind his relaxed attitude, Samantha sensed an uncanny alertness. The smooth suppleness of his stride suggested superb physical condition. Beneath the jacket, she guessed that the breadth of his shoulders tapering to a lean waist would confirm it.

The stranger stopped at the desk. "I'm looking for Samantha—"

A warning bell rang in her mind. "I'm Samantha Jones," she interrupted swiftly.

The man turned toward her at the sound of her clear voice. Instinct insisted that he had been aware of her watching him from the instant he walked through the door. She rose from her chair, the frankness of her gaze not wavering under the steady regard of his. Again with deceptive laziness, he smiled and walked toward her desk.

"The photograph on your father's desk doesn't do you justice, Miss Jones." There was the slightest inflection on her assumed name. The man spoke quietly yet firmly, as if he was unaccustomed to raising his voice. The iron thread of command was there without the need to shout.

Perhaps that was what had first tipped Samantha off to the fact that he had come to see Samantha Gentry and not Samantha Jones, the reporter. It was a trait her father looked for in his executives and associates. The reference to her picture on Reuben Gentry's desk seemed to confirm the stranger's connection with her father.

Samantha didn't recognize him, but that wasn't so strange. She knew very few of the people who worked with and for Reuben Gentry. Mostly they were faceless names.

"Your father?" Beth's voice echoed blankly from her desk. "I thought you said your father died two years ago, Sammi?"

For a fraction of a second, Samantha felt trapped by her own charade. "Yes, he did," she continued the white lie, calmly meeting the faint narrowing of the stranger's gaze. "But this man evidently knew my father."

"Yes, that's correct." The well-shaped masculine mouth, an underlying hardness in its line, twisted briefly as the man went along with her story.

Obviously he was bringing a message from her father, one he couldn't deliver in front of Beth, who believed Samantha's father was dead. Samantha reached for her handbag sitting beside her chair.

"Beth, we're going to the back room for some coffee," Samantha stated without satisfying the curiosity gleaming in the girl's eyes.

A table and folding chairs occupied the corner of a back room. A large coffee urn sat at one end of the table cluttered with clean and dirty paper cups and plastic spoons. It hardly resembled the plush boardrooms where Reuben Gentry held his meetings, but Samantha didn't even attempt to apologize for the ink- and coffee-stained tabletop. She walked to the urn and began filling one of the clean paper cups.

"I'm sorry, but I don't know you." Her gaze flicked briefly to the stranger. His veiled alertness was almost a tangible thing. "I assume Reuben sent you." It had been years since she had referred to her father as such.

"Owen Bradley, your fa—"

Samantha straightened. "You are Owen Bradley!" The statement came out smothered in an incredulous laugh. A dark eyebrow flicked upward in silent inquiry. Immediately she pressed her lips together and tried to stop smiling. "I'm sorry, I didn't mean to laugh. It's just that, well, you're not at all like I pictured Reuben's Man Friday to be."

Her frank brown eyes traveled over the man again, now identified as Owen Bradley, her father's secretary and general everything. Her image of Owen Bradley had been somewhat effeminate—a short, thin man perhaps with pale skin and thick glasses, highly efficient and a walking computer.

But this Owen Bradley, the real Owen Bradley, seemed to belong to the outdoors. His features were roughly hewn out of teak wood. There was nothing effeminate about him. Male virility was chiseled from the solid angle of his jaw through the faint broken bend of his nose to the smooth slant of his forehead.

At closer quarters, Samantha realized that his eyes were not dark brown as she had first thought. They were deep charcoal gray, like thick smoke, with the same obscuring ability to conceal his thoughts. There was nothing handsome about him, yet she felt some invisible force stealing her breath away.

Turning back to the coffee urn, she set another white cup beneath its spout. "Do you take cream or sugar?" The husky quality always present in her voice was more pronounced.

"Black."

"It's liable to be very black," Samantha warned. She handed the cup to him, noticing his large hands and the roughness of his fingers that suggested hard physical labor. "That's the way Harry likes it. Since he's the first one here in the mornings, that's the way he makes it, regardless of anyone else's preference." She added two spoonfuls of powdered cream to her own cup of the almost syrupy black liquid.

"I don't mind." And he sipped the potent liquid without the slightest grimace.

Samantha suppressed a shudder at the undiluted strength of the coffee he had just swallowed. Normally she preferred black coffee, too, but this wasn't really her idea of coffee.

"Have a seat." She gestured toward the dilapidated folding chairs.

The man named Owen Bradley chose one that put his back to the wall. His gaze scanned the room and corridor with lazy interest. Samantha doubted if he had missed any detail in that brief look.

"I was informed you had changed your name, Miss Jones, but I hadn't realized you'd killed your father off in the process." On the surface it sounded like an apology for his inadvertent reference to her father in front of Beth, but Samantha didn't think it really was.

"Only for the summer." Sitting in a chair opposite him, she absently smoothed the fold of her denim wraparound skirt. "It seemed easier than coming up with a fictitious background and activities for him as well as myself." Samantha wasn't entirely sure why she was explaining except that she didn't want her father's secretary thinking she had permanently disposed of her father even in her mind. "Why did Reuben send you instead of relaying a message through Harry?" Harry Lindsey, the editor, had been Samantha's communication link with her father.

"He tried, but Harry went out of town yesterday, so your father sent me up from New York."

"I'd forgotten about that." Belatedly Samantha remembered Harry's sudden departure from the office yesterday and his expected return at any moment. Then she tipped her head to one side, curiosity gleaming in her candid brown eyes. She wasn't surprised that her father hadn't attempted to contact her directly, but she did wonder why he had thought it necessary to send Owen Bradley to see her. "Is there something urgent?"

"Your father has arranged to have a couple of weeks free. He wants you to spend them with him," the quietly spoken voice informed her, not a flicker of expression chasing across his raw-boned features. "As Reuben put it, he wants you to spend one last vacation with him before you spread your wings and permanently leave the nest.''

That sounded like Reuben, Samantha thought with a sigh. Her fingers raked the thickness of the hair near her ears as she hesitated before responding.

Owen Bradley must have sensed the reason for her hesitation, because he said, ''A leave of absence can be arranged for your job. Harry never needed another full-time reporter on his staff anyway.''

Her temper flared for an indignant second. Initially Samantha had thought he was accusing her of being a spoiled and indulged rich girl whose daddy had created a job for her. But the dark smoke of his gaze was without censure. She checked her rising anger, giving Owen Bradley the benefit of the doubt. Possibly he was only reassuring her that she wouldn't be leaving Harry in the lurch.

''I could spend a week,'' she conceded, wanting to be with her father yet knowing the summer was short and wanting to gain all the experience working on the newspaper she could. ''Where's he going to be? Bermuda? St. Croix? Hawaii?'' she asked, naming his favorite vacation haunts.

''Thousand Islands,'' was the calm reply.

''Thousand Islands?'' Samantha repeated.

''Yes, near Clayton in upstate New York, the chain of islands in the St. Lawrence Seaway. He's rented a summer place on one of the islands,'' he explained patiently.

''I've heard of it.'' It would have been nearly impossible not to, because she had lived the majority of her twenty-two years in the state of New York.

The area had once been known as the millionaires' playground. Samantha suspected that her father had avoided it for that reason. Reuben Gentry rarely hob-nobbed with the so-called élite. He preferred being included in a gathering because of his merits as an individual and not the size of his bank balance. Now that it had become a simple vacation spot, she sup-posed he had decided to investigate it.

"Is there anything wrong?" Owen Bradley had been watching her turn over the information in her mind and now questioned the result.

"With his choice?" Samantha returned, then im-mediately made a negative movement of her head. "None. It just surprised me, but I should have learned to expect that from Reuben by now. When am I supposed to leave to meet him?"

"Today."

"What?" Her mouth opened.

"It's short notice," he agreed with a faint smile. "A couple of important meetings were postponed and Reuben took advantage of it to arrange some time off. I'm to drive you there today."

Samantha sighed. Once her father made a decision, he never wasted any time carrying it out, and this spur-of-the-moment vacation was no exception. She thought of the clothes she had to pack and the wash-ing she had been putting off until the weekend and all of her sportswear hanging in her bedroom closet at her father's apartment.

"You don't have to bother about packing any

clothes," Owen Bradley said, reading her thoughts. "Your father doubted if you would have the kind of clothes along that you would need, so he sent some clothes up this morning. Any personal items that were overlooked you can buy when we get there."

"He's thought of everything," Samantha mused, lifting her shoulders in a helpless shrug of compliance. "I suppose he's already there waiting for me."

"He'll meet us there the day after tomorrow, Saturday."

She had just lifted the paper cup to her lips when he answered. "Us?" she questioned, taking a quick sip. The cream hadn't improved the bitter flavor. "Is this going to be one of those half-business half-pleasure vacations?"

"Something like that," he agreed and finished his coffee.

Samantha did the same, but she couldn't contain a grimace of distaste. His charcoal gray eyes crinkled at the corners in smiling sympathy, but he didn't comment. As he straightened from the chair, she couldn't help noticing the bulky fit of his dark green blazer across his chest. It seemed a pity that a man with his muscular physique couldn't afford her father's tailor, but Samantha would have been the first to admit that there were more important things in life than clothes.

"It's about a six-hour drive to Clayton. If we leave now, we can make it before dark," Owen Bradley stated.

"Can't we wait until Harry comes back?" She frowned. "I'd like to explain...."

"I have a letter here for him." He removed a plain white envelope from the inner pocket of his jacket. "I'll leave it in his office while you freshen up before we go."

There were no more objections left to make. With a quiescent nod, Samantha rose. As they entered the corridor leading to the front offices she pointed out Harry Lindsey's private office and continued to her own desk as Owen Bradley stopped to leave the letter. Beth was instantly at her side.

"Who is he?" she whispered eagerly.

"A friend of the family." Samantha covered her typewriter and quickly began straightening her desk.

"Did you know him?"

"Not exactly. I knew *of* him." She handed the other girl the column she had completed just before Owen Bradley arrived. "Give this to Mr. Lindsey when he comes. There's been a family emergency and I have to leave."

"With him?" Beth's eyes rounded. "Are you sure it's safe? He looks kind of dangerous to me."

"He looks like a man to me," Samantha smiled. In her mind she put "man" in capital letters.

"Are you positive you know who he is?" Beth persisted in a low whisper. "Did you ask for any identification? Remember what your horoscope said: BEWARE OF STRANGERS."

"Oh, honestly!" Samantha laughed aloud this time. How could Beth take that nonsense seriously?

"It's just coincidence, I suppose, that your horoscope warned you about strangers this month and now a stranger that you think you've heard of walks in today," Beth declared in a wounded voice.

"That's all it is." Shaking her head at the disbelieving look in her co-worker's face, Samantha turned and gazed squarely at Owen Bradley standing silently in the hall opening.

There was a flash of white as he smiled. "Ready?"

"Yes," Samantha nodded, deciding that the only thing dangerous about him was the havoc he could wreak with her senses. That smile had increased her pulse rate and its charm had been directed at her only for a few seconds. It was a shame he worked for her father. Nothing would ever come of the attraction she could feel growing.

*Enjoy it while it lasts,* Samantha told herself. A series of pleasant interludes would probably be the only love life she would know. There was no sense shying away from the first potentially exciting male to come her way simply because the attraction was doomed to die.

Why not take advantage of the fact that it would be difficult for him to say no to the boss's daughter, especially when the boss was Reuben Gentry? But Samantha smiled at herself, knowing she would never take advantage of that fact, no matter how attractive she found a man.

## CHAPTER TWO

THE TELEPHONE POLES were whizzing by so fast that they looked as close together as fence posts. Samantha's hand tightened instinctively on the car door's armrest as they approached a curve in the highway. Centrifugal force pressed her against the door, but the car hugged the road all the way around the curve into another stretch of straight highway.

"Is someone chasing us, or do you just always drive this fast?" she murmured, half-jesting and half-serious.

"Sorry." Owen Bradley's gaze flicked to her absently, almost as if he had forgotten she was sitting in the passenger seat. For the past two hours, Samantha was nearly positive he had. His foot eased its pressure on the accelerator and the powerful car slowed to a speed closer to the posted limit.

"I didn't mean to frighten you by driving so fast," he apologized.

"Normally it doesn't bother me when it's on the divided highway of an interstate, but on these secondary highways with their curves and intersecions ...." Samantha left the rest unfinished.

It wasn't that she questioned his driving skill. It was

superb. She was certain he was probably in control of the sports car every minute. But it was some of the other idiots with licenses that she worried about meeting.

"True, but the secondary highways offer a much more scenic route," he replied.

Staring out the window at the rolling hills dotted with groves of trees and pastoral farms, Samantha silently agreed it was beautiful, especially now that it wasn't so much of a blur. She shifted to a more comfortable position in the seat and the dark gray eyes slid briefly to her again.

"Getting tired?" he inquired.

"Stiff from sitting," she acknowledged with a smile that said it was to be expected after more than four hours on the road. They had stopped once to refuel and she had stretched her legs then, but that had been two hours ago.

"There's a good restaurant in this next town. We'll stop there to eat," he told her.

More silence followed, but it wasn't really so bad, Samantha conceded. In fact, it was rather nice. Not that she wouldn't have liked to find out more about the real Owen Bradley now that she had met him. He had answered her general question readily enough at the start of their journey, but he hadn't volunteered any information she hadn't already heard from her father.

He had been disinclined to talk about himself and the conversation had drifted into generalities and finally into silence. Although she knew a lot of facts about Owen Bradley, the man remained an enigma in many ways.

His latent animal grace suggested a man with physical pursuits as well as mental. It was hard for Samantha to visualize him spending as many hours in boardrooms and offices as his position with her father demanded. He was in his middle to late thirties and unmarried—that fact had been relayed by her father because he had wanted someone at his beck and call and not tied down with family.

But had he never been married? His blatant masculinity would attract a lot of women; Samantha could feel its pull on her. Was he divorced or widowed? Or a confirmed bachelor like herself? She would find out the answers eventually. She wasn't training to be a reporter for nothing. As a matter of fact, she could find out the details from her father when she saw him on Saturday.

Three-quarters of an hour later, they were sitting in the restaurant, their meal eaten, and lingering over their coffee. Owen had asked her a couple of questions about her job with the newspaper, which she had answered.

"This coffee is a definite improvement on Harry's," she added after answering his questions.

With a smile, she glanced from her cup to his face. He wasn't looking at her but watching the activities of the various people in the restaurant. Their corner table gave him an unlimited view and he had been taking advantage of it ever since they had sat down, only occasionally glancing at Samantha.

His lack of attention irritated her. She was the boss's daughter and he could at least pretend to be interested in entertaining her. Samantha tipped her head to one side, seal brown hair falling around her shoulders.

"Am I boring you?" she asked with frank candor.

The unreadable dark smoke screen of his gaze turned to her, dark brown nearly black hair growing thickly away from his wide forehead. The well-molded mouth was slightly curved, a suggestion of hardness in the otherwise sensual line of his masculine lips.

"Not at all," Owen Bradley assured her in his low voice that never seemed to vary in volume.

Now that Samantha had begun, she wasn't going to turn back. "I wasn't sure you were paying attention to what I said," she commented honestly.

"That's not true. You were telling me about a feature article you were going to do on an elderly lady named Jane Bates who's celebrating her hundredth birthday, and your unique idea about having her discuss how women's attitudes have changed over the years and how it's affected her, if at all." Very concisely he condensed what she had told him.

"I stand rebuked," Samantha apologized wryly. "I thought you were thinking about something else."

"I never forgot for a minute that you were sitting beside me." He regarded her steadily for several disturbing seconds.

Samantha wasn't certain how she should take that—whether he meant that he wished he could have forgotten about her or that she had made too much of an impression for him to do so. She had the uncomfortable feeling he was indulging her.

"Do you have a sister?" she asked finally, bracing herself for the words that would sting. She had lost her immunity with him.

"No." Amusement gleamed briefly in his eyes. "But if I did, she'd probably look like me and not like you." Samantha blinked. He pushed his chair away from the table and rose. "The sun's going down. We'd better get back on the road."

Inside the car once more, Samantha didn't attempt to check her curiosity. Half turning in her seat, she studied the roughly carved profile for a thoughtful second.

"Why did you say that?" she asked.

"What?" The headlight beams were slicing through semidarkness of twilight. His gaze didn't flicker from the road.

"That I wouldn't look like your sister if you had one," Samantha answered evenly.

"It's true. But that isn't what you're really asking, is it?" He glanced into his rearview mirror before pulling into the other lane to pass the car ahead. "No one who has worked very closely with Reuben could fail to hear the comments made about him and his daughter."

"So you've heard me described as attractive in a sisterly kind of way," she concluded.

"I've met a lot of men and none of them had a sister that looked like you." The mocking glitter of his charcoal eyes held her gaze for an instant. The quiet voice was teasing her and Samantha laughed softly. A pleasant warmth invaded her limbs. The contentment she felt had nothing to do with a full stomach or the refreshing draft of outside air from the vent. She relaxed in the bucket seat and gazed out the window at the first evening star twinkling in the purpling sky.

The stars were out in force when they finally drove through the quiet streets of Clayton, New York. Unerringly Owen Bradley drove through the town, not stopping until he reached a docking area on the river front.

No boats were moored there, so Samantha assumed it was a place where boats simply took on or let off passengers. When Owen reached behind the seat for his briefcase and stepped out of the car, she followed suit.

The night's darkness had colored the river black, and the rippling current reflected the silvery beams of a crescent moon, creating an effect of silvery lace against black satin. The horizon was an indistinguishable mound of lumpy shapes.

A strange voice broke the gentle silence, causing Samantha to nearly jump out of her skin. "The boat will be here shortly."

Spinning to face it, she saw a man, as tall as Owen Bradley, standing beside him. The shadows of a building concealed his features from her gaze.

"Thanks, Bert," said Owen Bradley, who then handed the man something.

Evidently it was the car keys, since the man opened the driver's door and slid behind the wheel. He reversed the car and started back the way they had come. Almost instantly the sound of the car's motor was joined by that of a boat, its navigational lights approaching the dock.

Samantha's elbow was taken and Owen led her to the side of the street within the shadows of a building. "Wait here," he ordered firmly, and walked in long easy strides towards the river's edge.

A sailboat came into view, its canvas furled, an empty mast jutting into the darkness. At almost the same instant that the boat cut its power to come into the dock, Samantha heard the car stop at the corner. She glanced at it, seeing a woman step from the sidewalk and climb into the passenger side before it drove off. Bert whoever-he-was obviously had a girl friend, she thought, smiling to herself, and turned back to the dock.

A line was being tossed to Owen from the boat. With quick expert twists, he had it looped around a mooring pin and was signaling to Samantha to join him. An older, burly-looking man was on deck to offer her a steadying hand aboard. He was built like a football player, muscle-necked and barrel-chested.

"Thanks," she murmured, but the man was already disappearing to another part of the boat.

The line was freed and Owen stepped on deck. "You'd better go below while we get under way."

The night air was cool on the water. If Samantha had had a sweater to cover the bareness of her arms below the short sleeves of her blouse, she might have argued that she would rather stay on deck. Instead she went below without protest.

The boat's engines throbbed with power as they moved away from the dock. The lights of the town began to recede. Samantha doubted if two minutes had elapsed between the time the car had stopped at the dock and the boat had left.

There was a brief shake of her head as a bemused smile touched her mouth. Only Reuben Gentry could have organized an operation as efficient as this, with someone waiting to take the car and the boat probably waiting just beyond the dock.

Settling onto a cushioned seat in the cabin, Samantha rubbed her shivering skin to erase the chilling goosebumps. On deck, footsteps approached the stairwell to the cabin. A few seconds later Owen Bradley's tall frame appeared above.

"Comfortable?" he inquired with that lazy movement of his mouth into a smile. His briefcase was set on a nearby cushion.

"Fine," Samantha nodded, "although I wish I'd brought a sweater."

He glanced sharply at her crossed arms that gave her a faintly huddled pose. "I think there's a spare windbreaker around here that you can wear."

He walked past the galley area and disappeared from her view. She could hear him opening and closing doors in what was probably the sleeping quarters. For an instant, Samantha had thought he might offer her the use of his jacket. She smiled wryly. Such gestures of chivalry were usually confined to the motion picture screens. He certainly was familiar with the boat and its contents, though.

"Here you go." He reappeared, offering her a light blue windbreaker. Samantha quickly slipped it on, losing her hands in the long sleeves. It was several sizes too large, but it offered protection, and that was what mattered. "Sorry, but there wasn't anything smaller."

"That's all right." She rolled the sleeves back to her wrists and spared a glance out through the narrowed windows. But the glass reflected a dark picture of the interior of the cabin. "How much longer before we arrive at the island?"

"An hour, more or less," he shrugged blandly and moved toward the steps leading to the deck. He paused. "There's some coffee in the thermos. Help yourself." He gestured toward the galley to indicate its location. Warmth was briefly visible in his smoky gaze. "I can't guarantee it's better than Harry's, but it is hot."

"Thanks," Samantha smiled, and he disappeared up the steps.

The coffee turned out to be delicious. She curled both hands around the cup to let her cold fingers take advantage of its heat. Relaxing against the cushion, she leaned her head back and listened to the throb of the boat's engines. It seemed to be the only sound in the entire world, except for the occasional murmur of voices between Owen and the burly boatman above.

Almost inevitably it seemed, her thoughts became focused on Owen Bradley. In so many ways, he was a contradiction—for instance, his muscular physique and keenly intelligent mind. Not that the two couldn't go together, but Samantha had difficulty visualizing him as her father's secretary.

The position involved limited, nearly nonexistent physical activity. And there was that air of indolence he adopted to disguise his ever constant alertness. The air of idle distraction bordered on aloofness, yet he was aware every second of what was happening around him.

The quiet, low-pitched voice was always firm with purpose and authority. Something in its tone suggested that whoever decided to cross him should beware of the consequences. Behind the bland expressions and slow smiles lay an unrelenting hardness, a hint of ruthlessness stamped in the rough features.

It would be interesting and a challenge to find out what made him tick, Samantha decided. Swallowing the last of the coffee, she leaned back again and closed her eyes. His subtle compliment that Samantha didn't look like the sister of anyone he had known returned. She realized Owen Bradley was very adept at handling women, too.

One minute she had been irritated because he didn't seem to be paying any attention to her, and within the space of a few words, he had made her feel important and beautiful without uttering any extravagant compliments she would have doubted. He had to be aware of the impact his virility had on the opposite sex.

Yet it wasn't the direct assault that a strikingly

handsome man would make. It was a slow undermining that removed the ground from under a girl's feet and sent her toppling before she realized what was happening. That was the danger Beth had instinctively sensed, Samantha decided. Admittedly, he was a devastatingly potent combination.

The long drive had tired Samantha more than she had realized. She drifted into a state of half sleep, aided by the hypnotic throb of the engines. Her head bobbed to one side, waking her. She sat up straight, rubbing the side of her neck and chiding herself for dropping off like an old woman.

The steady rhythm of the engines altered its tempo. Stifling a yawn, Samantha glanced at her watch, but she couldn't remember what time they had arrived at the boat. She had the feeling that she had been dozing for much longer than it seemed. As she started to peer out of the narrow windows, footsteps again approached the stairs to the cabin.

"We're coming into the island now," announced Owen, coming halfway down the stairs.

"I'll be right there," Samantha answered.

Picking up her cup, she carried it to the galley sink and rinsed it out. As she started toward the steps, she noticed the briefcase sitting in the cushion and picked it up, glancing briefly at the initials. Her ascent to the deck was in time to catch a shadowy glimpse of rocks, trees and shrubs before the island was obscured by a solid wall of black that suddenly surrounded three sides of the boat and blocked out the night sky. It took her a full second to realize that they had glided silently into a boathouse. The engines were cut. In the dimness, Samantha could just barely make out the shapes of the two men making the boat fast as it rubbed against the side of the inner dock. A solitary light bulb was switched on when the boathouse doors to the river were shut. It cast more shadows than the darkness it illuminated.

After the incessant hum of the engines, the silence seemed eerie. Water lapped against the hull and the men's footsteps echoed hollowly on the boards of the dock. The boathouse seemed like an enormous cavern with its high walls and roof to allow the tall-masted sailboat within.

"Ready?" Owen Bradley's voice prompted from the dock.

Samantha moved toward him, accepting the steadying hand on her arm as she stepped from the boat deck onto the dock. The boat rocked slightly as she pushed off and she stumbled against him, the briefcase making her balance awkward. Immediately, his large hands spanned her waist to hold her upright. The hard length of him was imprinted on her hips and thighs.

Tipping her head back, Samantha started to make a self-deriding comment about her clumsiness, but the words never left her parted lips. The mesmerizing quality in his gaze stole her voice and breath. Her pulse tripped over itself in rapid succession. When his attention slid to her mouth, she was certain he was going to kiss her, and she held her breath in anticipation.

The grip on her waist lingered for several more seconds, then he firmly held her steady as he stepped back. Disappointment surged through Samantha. She tried to hide it with a shaky laugh and a change of subject.

"You should ask Reuben for a raise when he gets here on Saturday," she jested as if that moment of intimacy had never been about to happen.

His expression was immediately shuttered, yet there was considering alertness behind the lazy smile. "Why do you say that?"

"Because it doesn't suit his corporate image to have his secretary running around carrying a briefcase with someone else's initials," she answered as she offered the briefcase to him.

The expensive briefcase carried telltale marks of much use. Near the handle were two gold letters: C.S. Samantha had noticed them briefly when she had picked the case up from the cabin seat.

"I think Reuben can afford to buy you a briefcase with your own initials, Owen," she declared.

She hadn't placed any significance on the incorrectly initialed briefcase. If she had thought anything about it at all, it had been only an idle assumption that he had purchased it used because it was sturdy and durable, capable of taking the beating of travel and use that his position would demand.

He took the suitcase, glancing at the initials thoughtfully before meeting her smiling and unwary look. "I'd forgotten that as a reporter it's your job to notice things," he mused aloud. The smoke screen of his gaze made his thoughts unreadable as he paused. "I'm not Owen Bradley."

Samantha's brown eyes widened. "You said—"

"No, you said I was Owen Bradley," he corrected lazily. "I simply didn't bother to deny it. Actually what I had been going to say was that Owen Bradley had told me where I could find you."

"Then who are you?" she demanded with an accusing frown.

"Chris Andrews. The 'S' is for Steven, my middle name." His finger tapped the initials on the briefcase. "The 'A' was knocked off sometime or another."

"Chris Andrews?" Samantha repeated in disbelief. "*The* Chris Andrews?"

"I don't know how many you know." A mocking smile played with the corners of his well-shaped and firm mouth.

As far as Samantha was concerned, there was only one Chris Andrews. He wasn't exactly a rival of her father's, but they held competitive interests that often clashed. But Reuben Gentry admired his business and financial skills even when he cursed him. And like her father, he shunned publicity. Samantha couldn't ever remember seeing a picture of him.

"Does Reuben know you've brought me here?" she demanded, still trying to sort through the astounding revelation and find its true significance.

"Of course," Owen Bradley, who now turned out to be Chris Andrews, replied, nodding without hesitation. "I told you, he'll be here Saturday."

"Why?" She tipped her head to the side.

"Because I invited him," he returned blandly.

"This is your home?" confronted Samantha "Your boat?"

"Yes."

"Why am I here? And why is Reuben coming?" All of her reporter instincts rushed to the fore, and she sharply questioned his motives as she drew herself up to her full height of five feet six inches and still had to look up to see his face, raw-boned and unreadable.

"Reuben owns stock in some companies I have been trying to buy and he has been unwilling to sell. It's an amicable disagreement. I invited him here for two weeks in hopes of negotiating a compromise. He accepted, but I wouldn't attempt to guess at his reasons," the man who had identified himself as Chris Andrews replied.

"That still doesn't answer why I'm here," Samantha reminded him smoothly.

"You're here for the same reason I gave you at the newspaper. Reuben wants to spend some time with you before you fly away into the world. He asked if you could come and I agreed."

"Why would you agree? Wouldn't I be disrupting you from your purpose and distracting my father?" she accused.

"Possibly, but I'm willing to take the risk," he shrugged diffidently. "Besides, if having you here will put your father in a good mood, it might make the negotiations easier."

"What you mean is that my presence might make

him less resistant to your persuasions. I'm here to soften his stand, is that it?''

"And with luck to have a peaceful and relaxing week with your father," Chris Andrews added.

His logic was convincing her of the truth in his answers, however selfish the motivation was. But there was one point that Samantha still wanted to have clarified.

"Why am I here now? Before Reuben comes on Saturday?" she wanted to know, boldly meeting his veiled look.

"Obviously we've never met," he acknowledged the fact. "I thought it would be prudent to get to know you a bit beforehand to see which way the wind blew."

"In case I turned out to be an obstacle." She completed what he had left unsaid. "You'll find out, Mr. Andrews, that I don't even attempt to influence my father one way or the other when it comes to business matters."

"Then we all should have a very pleasant vacation. Especially if you started calling me Chris." The suntanned corners of his eyes crinkled as he smiled. "Shall we go to the house?"

His hand was raised in a gesture that indicated she should precede him to the door leading out of the boathouse. Samantha took an agreeing step and stopped, a question suddenly occurring to her.

"Why didn't you tell me who you were in the beginning? Why all this secrecy until now?" she demanded with another faintly defiant tilt of her head.

"If I told you at the newspaper office, I'm not certain you would have agreed to come with me. You might not have agreed to the vacation at all. When you mistook me for Reuben's secretary, I took advantage of it to get you here. Once you were here, I thought I would be able to persuade you to stay. Have I?" The dark head was tipped to one side, the glittering light in his eye mockingly asking to be forgiven for the harmless deception.

"If I said no, would you take me back?" Her eyes were bright. They had lost their accusing darkness as his explanations satisfied her without eliminating the trace of irritation she felt at being deceived.

"At this hour? I'm afraid not." His eyebrows slid upward. Chris Andrews knew she wasn't seriously expecting him to agree and his response was in the same light vein as her question.

"In that case, since you've succeeded in tricking me here, you might as well show me where I'm going to sleep tonight," Samantha declared in a sighing agreement that was only partially reluctant.

"This way." Again Chris indicated the door, standing to the side for Samantha to lead the way.

As she opened it and stepped into the night, the interior light from the boathouse revealed a path of dirt and bedrock worn smooth from frequent use. The light was switched off when Chris walked through the door.

Samantha stopped. "The man who was on the boat is still in there," she reminded him, knowing the boathouse would be pitch black without the one light.

"Tom? No, he left within minutes after we docked. He's at the house drinking coffee by now," he assured her, tucking a hand beneath Samantha's elbow to guide her over the path that was unfamiliar to her.

A light gleamed distantly through the thick stand of trees lining the path.

It appeared to be their destination as they wound along the trail through the trees. Samantha couldn't help reflecting on the day's events and the man whose hands so firmly guided her along. She was unaware of the soft laugh that escaped her curved lips until Chris Andrews asked in a tone of amused curiosity, "What's so funny?"

Samantha darted him a sideways glance, but little of the light from the stars and the sliver of the moon penetrated the dense tree limbs overhead. His craggy features were shadowed.

"Beth, the girl at the newspaper office, read my horoscope today for the month of June." Her smile deepened as she paused, considering her skeptical reaction to the forecast. It had been more like outright disbelief.

"Are you a follower of astrology?" His voice echoed her own previously held opinion that it was a great deal of nonsense.

"I haven't been, but after today, I might reconsider," Samantha conceded, the curve remaining on her mouth.

"Why after today?"

"Because my horoscope said to beware of strangers,

that they wouldn't be what they seemed," she explained with a short laugh. "It certainly turned out to be prophetic in this case. I was just becoming accustomed to the fact that you were Owen Bradley, a man I'd long pictured as being pale, short and thin, wearing glasses. Now I learn that you're really Chris Andrews and not Owen Bradley at all."

"I see what you mean." But the inflection of his voice didn't seem to find it as genuinely amusing as Samantha did, and she let the subject drop.

The house of native stone and wood was a rambling, one-story structure nestled in the trees. The spacious interior was designed with traditional simplicity. Although all the furniture was finely crafted, the casual atmosphere gave the impression that feet could be put up anywhere.

A tray of coffee and an assortment of cookies had been set near the sofa in front of the massive stone fireplace in the living room. A yawn rose in Samantha's throat as she tried to take another drink of her coffee. She covered the action quickly with the back of her hand, but not before Chris Andrews noticed it and suggested she would prefer her bedroom to more coffee.

"Maggie!" he called, and a tall blond woman appeared in the living room archway. "Would you show Miss Gentry her room?" he asked before introducing Samantha to Maggie Carlton, identified as Tom's sister.

The woman, in her mid-thirties, had inherited some of her brother's looks. She was pleasantly attractive, although some of her features were force-fully strong, almost intimidatingly so. There was keen intelligence in the blue eyes that met Samantha's smile with reserved friendliness.

Yet there was something that didn't seem quite right, and Samantha couldn't decide what it was. Maybe it was the look that Maggie Carlton had given Chris Andrews before she had shown Samantha to her bedroom. It wasn't exactly the type of look that would be exchanged between employer and employee. There was something more familiar in it that indicated a relationship more like the one Samantha had with Harry Lindsey, a friend of her father's and known to her long before she went to work for him this summer.

There was nothing wrong with a suggestion of friendship between the two, except that the age difference of Chris Andrews and Maggie Carlton was not as vast as the one between Samantha and Harry. Samantha didn't want to dwell on why that bothered her.

# CHAPTER THREE

It was nearly midday before Samantha wakened, a discovery that hurried her movements to dress. The bedroom closet was filled with sports clothes of every description, although the majority of them were decidedly casual and made for physical abuse.

Wearing a pair of wheat-colored denim pants and a matching tan and brown plaid blouse, Samantha hurried from her room into the hallway. A complementing gold scarf had been in a dresser drawer. She had folded it and used it as a hairband, the shimmering tails of the scarf partially lost in the rich seal brown shade of her dark hair.

Relying on her memory of the house's layout from the previous night, she retraced her way to the living room, then let instinct guide her to where the dining room should be located. Voices were coming from the room she had chosen as her destination. Samantha paused in the doorway to listen without being conscious that she was virtually eavesdropping.

Chris Andrews—she had readjusted her thinking to call him by his right name—was standing in front of a large picture window. Cream-colored slacks of a roughly corded material molded the muscular length of his legs. A windbreaker of navy blue covered most of a knit shirt in a lighter shade of blue.

But it was the expression on the roughly chiseled features that claimed Samantha's attention. It was hard and unrelenting as his gaze narrowed on the blond woman facing him.

"There won't be any discussion." The tone of his ominously low-pitched voice was clipped with command. "I don't like it any more than you do, but that's the way it stays."

Samantha must have made some involuntary movement at the chilling sound of his voice, because as Maggie Carlton started to protest with a grim voice, "But..." his narrowed gaze swung to the dining-room entrance and Samantha. A bland mask immediately covered his tanned features.

"Good morning. So you've finally decided to rejoin the living." The fine thread of mockery in his greeting held amusement. If Samantha hadn't witnessed the incident a second ago, she would never have guessed a controlled anger broiled beneath the easygoing surface Chris Andrews now displayed.

She considered excusing herself, but that would have meant silently admitting that she had overheard what had been a private and personal exchange. She decided to pretend that nothing was amiss as far as she was concerned.

"Good morning," she returned cheerfully and advanced into the room. "I can't remember the last time I slept so late. It must be the fresh air."

"Undoubtedly," Chris Andrews agreed, darting a

pointed glance at his so-called housekeeper.

Maggie Carlton turned to face Samantha and smiled. There was a tightness in the movement that suggested the other girl wasn't as adept at concealing her emotions as Chris Andrews was. "I'll bring you some coffee, Miss Gentry. Do you have any preference for breakfast?"

"No breakfast for me," Samantha refused. "Coffee will be fine for now, since lunch is barely an hour away."

"Are you sure there isn't something you would like? Toast? Or a sweet roll to tide you over to lunch?" he inquired with a lifted brow.

"Quite sure," Samantha said, nodding decisively.

Slipping her fingers into the front pockets of her denims, she walked nonchalantly to the large picture window, but her side vision caught the look exchanged between the two. It was more than a signal of dismissal for Maggie to leave. Somehow Samantha had the sensation that Chris Andrews was transmitting a message that everything was all right.

As Maggie left the room, Samantha concentrated on the scenery outside the window. Considering the spectacular view offered, it wasn't hard to do. Some time during her life she had probably seen pictures or brochures of the Thousand Islands area, but nothing had prepared her for the breathtaking beauty that unfolded beyond the window.

The unending expanse of the majestic St. Lawrence River reflected the electric blue color of the sky. Its stunning breadth resembled a lake, rather than a river. The vivid green of tree-studded islands dotted its length. On the island closest to view, still some distance away, Samantha could see the white boards of a building shining through partially cleared trees.

"It's quite a view, isn't it?" Chris was standing beside her, gazing out the window.

"I never dreamed it was like this," she murmured in agreement. "It's all so—" she searched for the words "—so unspoiled. Are there really a thousand islands?" From the window's view on this rocky knoll of their island she could see possibly five, varying in size from fairly large to very small.

"There are over seventeen hundred islands in the St. Lawrence, most of them privately owned." He pointed toward the north. "That far island is in Canadian waters."

"Over one thousand seven hundred." Samantha was still caught by the number. "That's unbelievable!"

"The largest island has more than a hundred square miles and the smallest is a rock and two trees. By government definition, an island is land surrounded by water with at least one tree. Without trees, it's considered a shoal." A lazy smile was directed at her. "Do you think there's a chance now that you'll enjoy your stay here?"

"I might even write up a travel article to put in the paper when I get back," Samantha laughed. Her enthusiasm for the time she would spend here was growing. It was no longer based mainly on being with her father.

"Do you swim?"

"Yes, why?" Samantha glanced up at him, an impish light dancing in her brown eyes. "Are you trying
to tell me that if I want to leave this island before my
father comes, I'll have to swim?"

"I had something else in mind when I asked."
There was silent laughter in his expression. "But I'll
go along with that thought, too."

"Why did you ask, then?"

"It's supposed to be warm this afternoon. This island is crescent-shaped, forming a sheltered cove
that's perfect for swimming. I was going to suggest we
make use of it this afternoon," Chris replied.

"Sounds wonderful," she agreed as Maggie reen-
tered the informal dining room with the coffee.

IT WAS more than wonderful. It was perfect, Samantha
concluded, as she rested a cheek on the back of her
hand. The sunbaked boards of the raft anchored in
the cove were warm beneath her. Her black swimsuit
was backless, exposing her skin to the burning rays of
the sun.

A tiny sigh of regret slipped out. An hour of swimming and diving in the cove, plus another hour sun-
ning on the raft—soon she would have to retreat to
the shade or risk turning into a boiled lobster.

Through the slit between her lashes, she could see
Chris sitting on the other side of the raft, muscles
bronzed and rippling in the sun. His gaze was slowly
sweeping the river, betraying an alertness in his otherwise relaxed pose. Only a few boats had ventured any-

where near the island. Chris had explained that the pleasure craft mainly stayed near the ship channel unless they were operated by people who knew the river and shoals well.

The ship channel could be seen from the island. Samantha had glimpsed several large freight ships gliding, silently it seemed from her distance, up the river toward their ports of call on the Great Lakes. It was an impressive sight to see them moving majestically in such a contrified setting along the international seaway.

As if feeling her gaze, Chris turned. Samantha didn't pretend she hadn't been studying his decidedly masculine physique. Instead she let her lashes rise more and smiled leisurely.

"Ready for another swim?" he asked.

"No," she sighed ruefully and levered herself onto her elbows, "but if I don't get in the water or the shade pretty soon, I'll be burned to a crisp."

Fluidly, he was on his feet, offering a hand as she started to rise. It was an impersonal grip that pulled her upright, firm and releasing her without lingering for any suggestive moments, although Samantha wished it had.

At close quarters, the sight of him clad in brown swimming trunks with a gold stripe at the side was disturbing her senses. He was so vibrantly male that the primitive urges had awakened within her. If Samantha hadn't already been aware of their existence, she would have been shocked. As it was, she tried to ignore the sensations.

His attitude this afternoon had been friendly, but it hadn't invited any gestures that might put their relationship on a more familiar level. Samantha wondered if it was because of Maggie Carlton or because he wasn't interested in her as a woman. Regardless of his comment that she didn't look like a sister, she hoped that wasn't what he had in mind.

With an over-the-shoulder, downward look, his glance told her to follow an instant before he dived cleanly into the water. Her shallow dive paralleled his course. She surfaced a few feet from him, treading water as she pushed the wet hair away from her face with one hand. The coolness of the water against her sun-warmed skin sent an uncontrollable shudder through her that clattered her teeth.

"It feels like an ice cube now," she said with a shiver.

"Want to call it a day?" he asked, raking fingers through the wet thickness of his own hair.

Samantha's answer was to strike out for the cove's shoreline. Within a few strokes, he was pacing beside her, powerful arms slicing effortlessly to draw him through the water. Samantha didn't attempt to race him; she knew she would soon be outdistanced. Even though she was a good swimmer, she was no match for him.

The physical exertion helped to ease the chill of the water, but the shivers returned the minute her feet touched bottom to wade ashore. The beach towels were lying on a large boulder near the shore. Chris was closer and he reached them first.

"I think you need this," he smiled indulgently, and unfolded a towel to wrap it around her shoulders.

The sun had warmed the thick terry-cloth material. As it encircled her shoulders, Samantha closed her eyes in silent enjoyment of the warmth. She clutched the front of the towel around her, as Chris began rubbing the material against her shoulders and upper arms.

Opening her eyes, she murmured in appreciation, "Mmm, thanks...that feels good!"

Without realizing it, she swayed toward him, partially the result of the massaging pressure of his large hands. Her head was tipped back to gaze at him, water glistening on her lips. His hands stopped their motion, but they didn't release her.

A magnetic current flowed between them, stopping time. There was an imperceptible tightening of the strong fingers on her shoulders as his head made a slight downward movement toward her lips, and Samantha's heart thudded in anticipation of his kiss.

A motorboat swept close to the island, throttling down to a low drone as it passed the cove. The charcoal gaze flickered to the sound, wavering for tantalizing seconds, then focused on the boat. He lifted his head, his hands resting impersonally on her shoulders again. The withdrawal was complete. When his gaze returned to her, there was nothing in it to suggest that for a few seconds he had intended to kiss her.

"Let's go up to the house so you can change into some dry clothes," he suggested.

One hand fell away as he stepped to the side. The

other slid between her shoulder blades to direct her toward the well-worn path. Disappointment was bitter on Samantha's tongue. She wasn't about to pretend that he hadn't been about to kiss her—not this time.

"You were going to kiss me, then stopped. Why?" she demanded, her innate candor demanding the same from him.

The pressure of his hand propelled her forward despite her stiff resistance. She thought he was going to ignore her question and would have repeated it if his gaze hadn't slid to her. The mocking light in the dark gray depths didn't completely mask the hard glint.

"Maybe I didn't like the idea of being observed." His gaze swerved pointedly to the boathouse.

Samantha followed it, spying the burly figure of Tom Carlton messing around with the canvas from a sail. He had been in the vicinity of the boathouse all the while they were swimming. But she didn't believe for a minute that his presence had anything to do with Chris's changing his mind and said so.

"Don't give me that line!" Her temper was igniting. "It was the motorboat going by that distracted you. And I don't believe you would care whether Tom or a bunch of strangers saw us. It was something else that made you change your mind. You're using them as an excuse."

They had reached a section of the path that wound through a thick stand of trees, concealing them from the view of anyone from the house or the cove. His hand stopped pushing her forward as he stopped. Samantha did, too, bristling with wounded pride. His fingers slid through the tangle of wet hair to the back of her neck.

"Don't be ridiculous." The smile he gave her was lazy and warm.

The magic of it momentarily held her captive. Samantha remained motionless as his head dipped toward her. The touch of his mouth on her lips was light and cool and broke the spell. She didn't want gentleness. Violently she twisted away, her eyes flashing fire.

"And don't you be patronizing!" she snapped, spinning to storm up the path toward the house.

"Wait a minute."

His hand grabbed her arm to force her to obey, his fingers digging through the towel into the tender flesh of her arms. She stopped, not trying to wrench free. She slid a freezing look of distaste to his hand, despising his touch with force equalling the one that had a moment ago desired his kiss.

"Let go of me!" she demanded coldly.

"Sam, I—" A fine thread of steel ran through his voice, a grim warning that Samantha interrupted.

"Reuben is the only one who calls me Sam. To everyone else I am Samantha or Miss Gentry—and that includes you, Mr. Andrews," she informed him with icy disdain.

Something she had said struck a sensitive chord. A muscle jerked in his lean cheek as he clenched his jaw to check a retort. The habit of observing people's reactions and pursuing their cause had already become too deeply ingrained for Samantha to ignore it.

"It's Reuben, isn't it?" she demanded grimly. "You're afraid of my father."

"I am not afraid of Reuben Gentry." She could hear the hardness of his low voice as he enunciated each word.

"Probably not in the usual sense that most people are," Samantha conceded, shaking her head. "No, you don't want to indulge in any dalliance with his daughter for fear of offending him." Sarcasm laced her voice. "Are you afraid I'll run to him and accuse you of—what's that delightful old phrase—trifling with my affections? If I did that, he just might get angry at you and never agree to sell you that precious stock you're so anxious to buy. What a story this would make!"

Her laugh was short and contemptuous. His other hand took a matching grip of her opposite shoulder. The bright fire of her gaze unflinchingly met the dangerous storm clouds gathering in his eyes, but she felt insulated from his fury, despite the punishing grip of his hands that threatened to shake her to pieces.

"Maybe I should spread the word of how you cower at the thought of my father," she continued caustically. "I bet it would amuse a lot of people to discover that you tremble at the prospect of his displeasure. You pretend to call the tune, but you're the one doing the dancing. If it wasn't so pitiful, it would be—"

She was jerked to his chest, his mouth smothering the rest of her sentence. With brutal force, his kiss ravaged her lips, inflicting pain. Neither resistance nor response occurred to her. Her only thought was to survive the cruel assault of her senses.

She was caught in the thunderous storm of his male dominance. The reverberating roll of her heartbeat was loud in her ears. Lightning flashed through her veins, carrying a searing exhilaration of fear and excitement. But the punishing kiss had been obtained by arousing his anger, so there was no satisfaction in the crush of his hard embrace.

The iron bands of his fingers kept her trapped against his muscular length as he lifted his head. Feeling beaten and bruised, the sigh that escaped her throbbing lips was one of defeat rather than relief.

"That was what you wanted, wasn't it?" The cold steel of his eyes was impossible to hold.

"No." Samantha shivered uncontrollably, and this time it wasn't from the chilling swim. Her gaze slid away from his face. "No, it wasn't what I wanted."

He didn't try to stop her when she pushed herself out of his arms. The towel slipped and Samantha pulled it tightly around her, wanting to huddle into the rough material. She couldn't explain, not without admitting how much he had hurt her, first with his chaste attempt at a kiss and then with the latent degradation of the second kiss. She had the family pride, if not her own, to uphold. Squaring her shoulders, she lifted her chin.

"No, it wasn't," he said.

It took her a second to realize Chris was agreeing with her earlier assertion. The harshness had left his voice, causing her to glance at him warily. He seemed vaguely bemused.

"Aren't you afraid I'll run to Reuben and tell him the way you treated me just now?" she accused.

"You aren't the type to run to your father. You're as independent and self-sufficient as he is," he said with absolute certainty. "I guessed that all along."

Mystified, Samantha stared at him. "If you weren't afraid I would cause trouble for you with Reuben, then why didn't you kiss me?" She challenged him to prove his statement.

"But I did kiss you," he answered complacently, admitting with a slight shrug, "more roughly than I originally intended, but you have only yourself to blame for that. Your tongue has barbs."

"I don't understand." Samantha shook her head, not quite believing him. "That doesn't explain what stopped you before."

"I told you—I wanted more privacy. Come on." His hand slipped under her elbow, turning her toward the house. His attitude indicated that he had no intention of discussing it any further. "Let's go to the house."

Samantha bit her lip, more questions arising from his answer, but she sensed this time he would ignore them. He had said all he was going to say. Instinct told her that she wouldn't be able to rile him a second time regardless of her persistence. He was firmly in control and she doubted her ability to shake his hold.

Instead, she silently let him direct her toward the house, mulling over the answer he had given her to see if she could find any credence in it. Privacy, he had told her, supposedly because of Tom's watching. Yet Samantha knew that it had been the motorboat that had distracted him. Perhaps the distraction had reminded him that Tom was in the vicinity.

But why should that matter? Chris Andrews didn't seem the kind of man who would care what others saw or thought of his actions. Unless—a possibility glimmered—unless Tom would have related what he saw to his sister Maggie. Perhaps that was what concerned Chris and made him withdraw.

Was Maggie his mistress, his lover? It was certainly plausible even if she wasn't startlingly attractive. And there had already been one disagreement between them—Samantha had overheard part of it that morning. Had it been over her? Was Maggie jealous because he had a young female guest in the house, someone who would be entitled to his attention?

It was very likely. What was it Chris had said—that he didn't like it any more than Maggie did, but that was the way it had to be. Yes, because that was the way Reuben wanted it. He had specifically asked for Samantha to be invited. Chris could hardly refuse.

There was a dejected curve to her mouth as she reached the conclusion. She regretted the instinct and training that had refused to let the incident rest until she had discovered the reasons behind it. He had kissed her, yes, because she had expected it, invited it. Being the perfect host, he had obliged. Ruthlessly he would use anyone and anything to get what he wanted.

"Damn!" Samantha swore silently in bitterness. Why was it she was always attracted to the men who ended up only wanting something from Reuben Gentry? Her identity as an individual always seemed to get overshadowed by her position as his daughter. She had thought she had accepted that, but now she realized she hadn't.

Chris Andrews had made her resentment of her situation rise even higher than before. Whatever had made her think that he was any different than the other men she had known?

He wanted to use her to accomplish his own ends just as all the others did.

The knowledge erected a barrier. Behind it, Samantha remained outwardly friendly and congenial, going along with suggestions he made to entertain her the rest of the afternoon and evening, but making sure there was never any opening for intimacy. If he had noticed the difference in her behavior, he didn't indicate it. And Samantha went to bed that evening confident that she had restored her pride and self-respect.

When she entered the living room the following morning en route to the dining room for breakfast, she saw Chris seated at a desk located in a far corner with walls lined with shelves, a mock study area in the large room. A black telephone receiver was in his hand. He glanced up as she entered, recognition replacing the look of total concentration in his expression.

"I'll let you talk to her yourself," he said into the

mouthpiece before covering it with his hand. "It's your father," he told Samantha. "Something unexpected has come up and he won't be able to come until the first of the week. He wants to be sure you're all right and won't mind waiting until then for him to come. I told him you wouldn't mind, but I think he'd rather hear it from you." There was something faintly mocking in his tone.

Did Chris think she would welcome more days spent alone with him, Samantha wondered as she walked to the phone. He was probably so conceited that he thought she hadn't guessed the falseness of his attention. In his arrogance, he probably thought he was playing her along very expertly. But she wasn't a toy to be used and discarded.

Putting those thoughts aside, Samantha took the phone from his hand and said with determined brightness, "Hello, Reuben."

"How are you doing, Sam?" came the response.

She smiled a bit wryly. "I'm surviving." Chris Andrews leaned negligently backward in his chair. Yet every fiber sensed the intensity with which he listened and watched.

"Sam, I'm sorry about this delay. Believe me, if I—"

"You don't have to explain," Samantha interrupted. She read through his concern and heard the faint preoccupied air in his voice, a telltale sign that he was engrossed in some weighty and no doubt serious problem. She had long ago learned that her father rarely postponed anything unless there was a crisis looming. "I know you're doing everything you can," she assured him. "And don't worry about me. It's lovely here and I know Chris will keep me entertained until you come."

"Chris?" Reuben Gentry echoed blankly.

"Yes, Chris," Samantha laughed. He had sounded miles away, thinking of other things.

"Oh, yes, Chris, of course," he said as if it had suddenly dawned on him whom she was talking about. "Everything will be fine. You just mind what he tells you," he added absently.

An incredulous smile curved her mouth. It must have been some problem he had on his mind. He sounded as if he had forgotten she was twenty-two and able to take care of herself. But it was at times like these that she found him the most lovable. He aroused the maternal instinct in her.

"Of course, Reuben," she agreed in the same tone of voice she had used when she was nine. "Did you want to speak to Chris again?"

"No, it won't be necessary. Take care, Sam."

"Yes. I'll be seeing you, Reuben." They never said goodbye to each other. It was a habit they had begun when Samantha was a small child and had cried unceasingly whenever he got ready to leave on a business trip. He had made a pact with her not to say goodbye because he would always be back. It had struck some childish logic in her that enabled Samantha to let him leave without tears.

A smile lingered, faintly dimpling the corners of her mouth. She was aware of Chris's speculating look as she replaced the receiver back onto its cradle.

"Everything all right?" Chris asked, rising as Samantha turned toward the dining room.

"Fine," she answered smoothly without glancing around. "It's just as you said. Something rather important has come up to delay him."

There wasn't any need to mention that Reuben's preoccupied manner indicated that it was a very serious problem. It wasn't any of Chris's business, especially since she didn't know the nature of it. It might concern something that would be of benefit to her father's rival company.

"You and your father are very close, aren't you?" He pulled a chair away from the table in the dining room as he made the comment.

"It's always been just the two of us since I can remember," agreed Samantha. "I enjoy being with him. Lately, with college and work, I haven't been able to be with him as much as I'd like." Which was the truth, but she was adult enough to realize it was part of growing up.

"You admire your father a lot, don't you?" Chris sat in a chair on the opposite side of the table.

"Of course." Samantha sensed it wasn't an idle remark. "Why?"

"I was just thinking it would be difficult for a man to compete with your father."

A pitcher of orange juice sat on the table. Samantha filled two glasses before glancing up to meet his hooded look. It was on the tip of her tongue to say that she didn't expect a man to compete with her father. "Yes," she agreed out of obstinacy, "few men can compare with Reuben Gentry."

A grimness entered his features and satisfaction ebbed slowly through her. She hoped somewhere in his personality there lingered a bit of inferiority. Maybe he wouldn't be so sure of his ability to attract her.

# CHAPTER FOUR

PUNCHING THE FLUFFY PILLOW, Samantha snuggled her head into the hollow made by her hand and closed her eyes. For several seconds she lay motionless in the bed. Then she opened her eyes with an impatient sigh. It was no use; she simply wasn't sleepy.

Her hand fumbled over the bedside table until she found the light and switched it on. Her watch was beside the light. Samantha picked it up, sighing again when she saw it was a few minutes before midnight. She had been tossing and turning for the past hour and a half and she wasn't any nearer falling asleep than when she had first laid down.

The covers were thrown back as she slipped out of bed. A book was lying on the dresser, but she felt too restless to read. A walk seemed the better answer. Stripping, she changed into dark blue denims and a dark green and blue plaid blouse. The light blue windbreaker Chris had loaned her during the boat trip to the island was hanging beside the hooded sweatshirt she took from the hanger, and she made a mental note to remember to return it to him as she slipped on the sweatshirt and zipped the front.

Her canvas shoes with their rubber soles made no

sound on the carpeted floor. She moved stealthily down the corridor, through the living room and into the dining room, not wanting to awaken anyone in the silent house. She carefully slid the patio doors open and stepped into the cool of the night.

The silvery light from a crescent moon softly illuminated the rocky clearing that provided the house with its view of the river. She started forward, a destination in mind. A flashlight would have been useful, but Samantha didn't have any difficulty finding the path through the growth of evergreens, sprinkled with oak and maple.

It was not as well worn as the one leading to the boathouse but still easy to follow even in the night's shadow. Samantha had discovered it that morning when she had explored the island. The path led to the convex side of the crescent-shaped island where a gazebo had been built near a rocky promontory overlooking the river. The gazebo was Samantha's destination.

The island, she had discovered, was much larger than she had suspected, being several hundred yards wide and two or three times that long. It could have easily accommodated two homes without either of them aware of the other, but there was only one with its private boathouse and gazebo.

The small circular structure was ahead of her, gleaming whitely in the moonlight. The scrolling wood trim of the overhang and around the wooden railing gave it a dainty look. In the starshine, with the shimmering silk of the silent river flowing by, it looked enchanted. Samantha's restlessness vanished under its spell.

Sitting crosswise on the wooden seat inside the railing, she leaned a shoulder against a supporting post and hooked her arms around one knee, stretching the other leg out on the bench seat. Her wristwatch was still on the table beside the bed and she had no idea how long she sat there, drinking in the serenity, thinking about a multitude of things, none of them very important.

She could have stayed there all night, but the breeze off the river became more cool than refreshing. Flipping the hood of her sweatshirt over her head, she lingered for several more minutes before the invading chill drove her to her feet. A yawn claimed her as she reluctantly turned to retrace her path. It brought a lazy smile to her lips. At least that was a good sign that she might sleep when she got back.

With the hood covering the seal brown of her hair and her hands tucked in the slanted pockets of the sweatshirt, she strolled unhurriedly toward the house. A night bird cried in the stillness, the only sound to herald her return.

Carefully Samantha slid the patio door open and stepped inside, freezing when a low voice snarled behind her, "I wouldn't make a move if I were you!"

Instantly the room was flooded with light from an overhead fixture, momentarily blinding her. Her hand went up instinctively to shield her eyes from the unexpected brilliance.

"What's going on?" Alarm and astonishment mingled in the breathed question, the hood of her sweatshirt sliding a few inches back as she jerked her head away from the light.

"Sam!" The identification was made in a mixture of anger, exasperation and relief. "What are you doing wandering about at this hour?"

The recognition of Chris Andrews's voice turned her around. "I couldn't sleep." Her eyes were just beginning to focus properly. She was certain she had seen dark metal in the hand that was just sliding out from the inside of his jacket. A gun?

He was shaking his head in wry amusement, his gray eyes running over her. She could almost see the tautness leave him as he adopted an indolent stance.

"Tom!" His voice was directed to the open patio door that Samantha hadn't a chance to close. His hands were on his hips and his gaze never left her although his head turned slightly. "It's all right. It's Miss Gentry."

"Miss Gentry?" came the muffled reply of astonishment before the burly man stepped into the light shining on the patio. "How did she...?"

The question wasn't finished as Tom Carlson saw the way Samantha was staring at the revolver in his hand. He quickly tucked it inside his jacket, breaking her trancelike stare.

"I swear I didn't steal a thing!" she laughed, raising her hands in a mock gesture of fear and surrender as she turned to Chris once more. "I only went for a walk."

A throaty chuckle joined her laughter. "Well, you can't blame us for being cautious," Chris pointed out. "Isolated homes are ideal for burglars, although they generally prefer them to be unoccupied. We've only been here a few days, so they might not have known that. I hope we didn't frighten you too badly."

"Just for a few seconds," she admitted, able to smile now at the way her heart had stopped beating.

"I'm sorry, but we—" Chris began.

He was interrupted by Maggie Carlton calling something. Samantha understood the rest of what she said as her voice drew nearer.

"She isn't in her—" A harried-looking Maggie stopped in the archway between the living room and dining room, staring in disbelief at Samantha.

"—in her room?" Chris finished the sentence. "No, Miss Gentry couldn't sleep, so she went for a walk. She's the one Tom heard prowling around outside."

The blonde's gaze skittered almost guiltily away from his face to Samantha. Smiling tightly, she walked into the room where they were, her hands nervously reknotting the belt of her quilted robe.

"You gave us quite a scare, Miss Gentry," she declared with a hollow laugh.

"And vice versa," Samantha returned.

"After all this excitement, I don't think any of us can go back to sleep right away," Chris said. There was nothing rumpled about his appearance to indicate that he had ever been in bed.

"Maggie, why don't you fix us all some chocolate?"

"Of course," the woman agreed after a slight hesitation.

"Want some help?" Samantha offered.

"I can manage," Maggie assured her, and walked toward the kitchen.

Shaking the hood from her head, Samantha unzipped her sweat jacket against the prevailing warmth of the house and took it off. Tom closed the patio doors and moved toward the table to sit in one of the chairs. Samantha followed suit.

"Where did you go?" Chris straddled a chair, leisurely resting his hands on the straight back.

Samantha told him and they spent a few minutes idly discussing the benefits of a late-night walk. Then Maggie reappeared with the mugs of hot chocolate. By the time Samantha finished hers, she had already begun to feel its calming effect. That and the discovery that it was already nearly two in the morning made her drowsy.

With a tired "good night" to the trio seated at the table Samantha started for her room. Halfway there, she remembered she had left her sweatshirt on the chair.

A few steps into the living room she heard Chris say, "I'd like to know how she got out of the house with none of us hearing her."

Samantha hesitated. She was tired and didn't want to become involved with any more rehashing of the incident. With a shrug, she turned back toward her room. The sweatshirt could stay there until morning.

A knock on the door awakened her the next morning. Frowning her resentment at the intrusion of her sleep, she peered through her lashes at the sunlight peeking through the closed curtains.

"Who is it?" Samantha grumbled without stirring from her exceedingly comfortable position.

"Rise and shine." The door opened and Chris Andrews stood in its frame, tall and vital, looking as if he had had eight hours' sleep, which Samantha was sure was impossible.

"What time is it?" she mumbled, running a tired hand through her tousled hair and rolling onto her back, pulling the covers with her.

"Nearly ten," he answered.

Eight hours was almost possible, she conceded, although he looked as if he had been up for hours. Her sleepy eyes focused on his leanly muscled shape. Snug-fitting denims of faded blue covered the length of his legs. A yellow windbreaker, the zipper hooked at the bottom, covered most of the blue chambray shirt opened at the throat.

"I feel as if I've just gone to sleep." Her mouth was all cottony, adding to the naturally husky pitch of her voice.

"No worse for last night's adventure?" he inquired with a mocking lilt.

"I don't think so." Samantha's head made a negative movement on the pillow. Her sleepy brain suddenly realized he must have had a purpose in wakening her. "What do you want?"

"I thought we'd go sailing today. Since you've

never been here in the Thousand Island area of New York before, I decided it would be a good idea to show you around. There isn't any better way to see it than by boat. Are you game?" He tipped his head to one side in mocking challenge.

The suggestion sounded good even in her half-awake state. "Of course," she agreed. "Just give me half an hour to wash the sleep away and dress."

"You've got half an hour. Coffee's waiting in the dining room and Maggie is packing us lunch. The boat's ready as soon as you are," he concluded, reaching out to close the door.

Three-quarters of an hour later, the boat had left the shelter of the cove. The sails were raised and the motor turned off. Tom Carlton had come along to crew, a fact that momentarily surprised Samantha. It must have shown on her face, because Chris had explained almost immediately that sailing around the many islands through various small channels could be tricky with the changing currents.

Samantha decided it was probably best he was along as she covertly studied Chris Andrews at the helm. A breeze was ruffling the thickness of his dark hair. The ruggedness of his sun-bronzed features was disturbingly compelling in this setting of earth and sky and water. Lusty and virile, he was in his element. The sharpness of his gray eyes was far-seeing, like the eagle's.

All of it combined to heighten the physical attraction Samantha felt, despite a common sense that told her it was futile and possibly dangerous. She was here as Reuben Gentry's daughter and not simply as a female named Samantha. Maybe Tom Carlton's presence would help to remind her of that. The tour was to keep Reuben's daughter from being bored.

The charcoal gaze swung to her and Samantha pretended to be looking at a landmass beyond him. She felt the sweep of his gaze run over her from head to toe and knew she looked fresh and nautical in her white slacks, navy top and white scarf for a headband. Dark curling wings escaped the scarf to wave across her forehead.

"Are you awake now?" There was chiding amusement in his tone.

"Very much so. This is beautiful." Her enthusiasm was entirely false. "Is that Canada there?" she asked, waving a hand toward the landmass she had supposedly been studying.

"It's a Canadian island, yes, but not the mainland."

"Aren't we going to follow the ship channel?" she asked. They were steering an easterly course, but they were a considerable distance from the large ocean liner moving upriver.

"The Seaway Channel is mainly on the American side. I thought I'd show you the Canadian side first, the Admiralty and Navy groups of islands, so you could get an idea of the natural beauty to be found before we take in some of the man-made splendor of the American Islands," Chris explained, the line of his mouth twisting wryly.

Samantha spent a few minutes studying the sapphire water and the emerald islands. "It certainly is beautiful," she absently repeated.

"The Indians referred to this area as the 'Garden of the Great Spirit.' The early French explorers gave it the name we know it by—'Les Mille Iles' or the Thousand Islands. The St. Lawrence River was an Indian highway. They called it the 'River Without End,' which wasn't exactly true as far as boats were concerned because the rapids kept it from being navigable."

"What's the difference between the St. Lawrence River and the St. Lawrence Seaway?" Her reporter's instincts to discover all the facts went to work.

"The river has always been here, but the seaway is an inland water route, about 2,300 miles long, stretching from the Gulf of St. Lawrence to Lake Superior, connected by a series of locks and canals, including the seven-lock system needed to lift ships up the Niagara escarpment."

"Fantastic!" Samantha murmured.

"Ships from all parts of the world travel the waterway system," he added. "It was accomplished by the combined efforts of the U.S. and Canadian governments. Have you ever stopped to think that the border between Canada and the United States is the longest undefended border in the world?" There was a quick flash of a white smile being directed her way.

Her head bobbed negatively. "No, I don't think I have thought about it quite that way."

As the boat glided silently through the waters, with the loudest noise coming from the billowing of the

sails, Chris gave her a brief sketch of some of the
area's history during the early wars, mentioning the
War of 1812 and the Patriot War of 1837 when the
steamer *Sir Robert Peel* was sunk in the American
channel. All the while, they cruised slowly by islands of varying size, some without signs of habita-
tion and others with cozy bungalows amid the trees.

"This area was a natural during the rum-running
days of Prohibition. It was easy enough for smugglers
to dodge customs boats with all these islands to disap-
pear between. One island became so infamous as a
place to stash bootleg whiskey that it's known as
Whiskey Island." The Admiralty group was behind
them now, and Chris pointed to the left, indicating
the buildings on a jutting point of land. "That's Gana-
noque, Ontario, on the mainland of Canada. It's a
very picturesque town."

"Are we stopping there?" Samantha asked, warm-
ing to the idea of wandering through the streets.

"We won't have time."

He did swing the boat close enough to allow her a
tantalizing glimpse of the village. A tour boat was
docked at the harbor, making her wish she was one of
the passengers, but Chris was already turning the sailboat toward an open expanse of water, and she didn't
have time to dwell on the town.

He was talking again, explaining that while most of
the island homes she saw were strictly summer resi-
dences there were permanent inhabitants, such as the
one on the island they were approaching—Grindstone
Island, en route through the Navy group of Canadian

islands. They were mainly farming communities, he said, adding that they had once been dairy centers. Grindstone Island used to make its own cheese, called, appropriately, Grindstone cheese, but now they had switched mostly to cattle.

"They have their own elementary-school system, which the children attend until the seventh or eighth grade. Then they have to go to the mainland for the rest of their education, usually staying with friends or relatives during the school year."

"Talk about leaving the nest early!" Samantha smiled.

"How about going below and breaking out that picnic lunch Maggie packed?" Chris suggested. "I don't know about you, but I'm getting hungry."

"You?" she laughed. "I haven't even had breakfast, only coffee."

"Don't be too long or you'll miss the scenery," he called after her.

When Samantha returned with the sandwiches and cold beer, Tom took his to the forward part of the boat and ate alone. Samantha wondered if he was just naturally antisocial or simply a well-trained employee. She rarely noticed him watching her and Chris. He seemed more interested in the other boaters on the river than the fresh, unspoiled scenery. Of course, he was probably quite used to it. For her, it was an all new experience. She had never seen anything quite like it before. Munching contentedly on the halved roll layered with slices of ham and cheese, she pitied the person who looked on this with jaded eyes.

A sideways glance at the man at the helm tried to judge his reaction, but the carved bronze features only revealed intense concentration as he negotiated a narrow channel between two islands. Considering his knowledge of the area, it was something he had seen many times.

Dressed as he was, it was difficult to remember he was Chris Andrews, entrepreneur, financier, tycoon. He certainly didn't look like any ordinary working person, but neither did he fit the image her mind associated with the name Chris Andrews. Before she had met him, Samantha would have visualized Chris Andrews going sailing in snappy white ducks and a blazer with a captain's hat instead of going bare-headed with the wind ruffling his hair and wearing faded denims and a windbreaker.

Samantha much preferred this Chris Andrews to the one of her imagination. Then she pulled herself up quickly at the thought.

*Careful*, she warned herself. *Remember you're only here because he wants something from Reuben.* The sandwich lost much of its flavor.

Through the Navy group, their course took them to the Canadian channel. A tall white tower off the starboard bow beckoned to them. Samantha was told it was the Skydeck complex on Hill Island and it offered a lofty and panoramic view of the area. A section of the Thousand Island bridge system came into view with the islands used as stepping stones to span the river.

Chris pointed out the maze of islands, the area

known as Lost Channel. During the early wars, the pirate days and the Prohibition era, it had been often used by men knowledgeable about the area to lose their pursuers.

After they had sailed beneath the bridge, Chris instructed Tom to lessen the amount of canvas offered to the wind and their pace was slowed. Samantha glanced at him curiously.

He met her look and announced simply, "The Palisades."

Glancing ahead, Samantha saw the rocky cliffs they were approaching. Craggy and steep, they rose from the placid river to loom above the boat gliding by. The slashed, sharp stone of their faces was tinged with pink. The silence of the sail made their intimidation more profound and their harsh beauty more awesome.

As they passed the town of Rockport on the Canadian side, Chris began an arcing course to take them to the opposite side of the river. His smile to her was brief and slightly cynical.

"Now for that man-made splendor I told you about—the millionaires' playground," he said.

It wasn't along before Samantha knew what he was talking about. The islands she had seen up to now had been raw wilderness with rustic bungalows, but now as they approached the American channel, the islands and their homes began to change. The heavy brush and thick foliage of the trees that filtered the summer sun's rays to the virgin soil began to give way to expensive, manicured lawns, green and lush. The summer homes were now nearly palatial vacation villas for the rich. Not satisfied with the ornamentation of nature, the owners had statues and flower gardens adorning the lawns. The architecture of some of the homes took Samantha's breath away. There was beauty here, too, but a direct contrast to what she had seen before.

When they had passed through the Summerland group, Chris said, "The granddaddy of them all is coming up. Or it would have been," he qualified cryptically. "You've heard of Boldt Castle, haven't you?"

"Yes," Samantha answered hesitantly, trying to remember what she had heard about it and finding her recollection hazy. "Something about a castle a man built for his wife."

"Yes, George Boldt was his name," he said. "His was one of those Horatio Alger, rags-to-riches stories. He immigrated to this country around the time of the Civil War, eventually made his fortune sevral times over. He came here with his wife in the 1890s when this was an élite resort area for the very wealthy. As a boy in Europe, he had seen the castles along the Rhine and it was always his dream to own one. When he and his wife saw Hart Island, which at the time was shaped roughly like a heart, he decided to buy it and make his dream come true. Evidently he was quite a romantic, because he went to considerable expense to complete the shape of the heart and renamed it Heart Island. Then he began building his castle. He envisioned a whole colony with several buildings and the capability of entertaining a hundred guests and their servants. Marble, tapestry, silks, rugs, all were imported to furnish his castle. He had spent over two million dollars on it when his wife died. All work was stopped at her death and it was never completed."

Towers, medieval and grand, jutted above the treed island ahead. As the boat drew nearer, the castle itself began to take form. Tourists wandered about the island and tour boats were tied up at its dock.

"Has it been restored?" asked Samantha.

"No. When the work was stopped, thieves and vandals stole or destroyed most of the valuable goods. For years, it was abandoned to the bats and birds and insects. It's virtually a ruin now, with only a few of its four hundred rooms that can be viewed by the public. At today's inflated prices, it would probably take twenty fortunes to make Boldt's dream a reality." Chris paused, frowning slightly. His narrowed gray eyes focused on the turrets rising above the trees. "Now it's a romantic symbol of a dream that became empty without the love of a man's wife."

Crazily there was a lump in her throat as Samantha felt herself gripped by the tragic and poignant story. It was silly to be moved by it and she tried to shake away the sensation and view the place objectively. A family of tourists was wandering along the dock.

"Let's stop," she suggested eagerly.

His gaze swept over the island and the strolling clusters of people. Then with an abrupt, resolute shake of his head, he said, "No. We don't have time."

Samantha glanced at her watch. "Granted, it's after two, but surely we can stop for a half an hour," she argued.

His gaze sliced to Tom standing near the middle of the port-side deck. The burly man had clearly been able to hear her request and the negative answers she had received. His expression was grim as he met Chris's look, then he scanned the other boats slowing to view the castle. Only a few seconds had passed.

"I'm afraid not," Chris refused again. His mouth curved into a smile, but it didn't ease the unrelenting and forbidding set of his features. "Maybe another time."

Shrugging an acceptance, Samantha glanced away, focusing her puzzled brown gaze on the tall boat-house buildings opposite Heart Island. She was consumed by the strangest feeling that even if the whole afternoon was before them, Chris would still have refused to put ashore.

It didn't make any sense. He was making a special effort to take her on a tour of the Thousand Island area, yet he seemed to be restricting the tour to the boat deck.

With half an ear, she listened to the commentary he began as the sailboat swept gracefully by the castle. Her eyes noted the stately buildings of the Thousand Island Club, more elegant summer homes of noteworthy people, the island known as Devil's Oven that had once been the hiding place of a notorious pirate, the towering American span of the international bridge, the Rock Island Lighthouse, which was no longer in use, and the Thousand Island Park, but none of it claimed her interest.

The town buildings of Clayton prompted her to make one last test of her theory, especially when Chris mentioned the museum there.

"I don't suppose we'll have time to stop there, either."

The faint challenge in her tone drew the swift appraisal of his charcoal eyes, the speculation in their narrowed look not quite hidden.

"Not this time," he answered without elaboration.

Not ever. The premonition was so strong it nearly was spoken. The force of her certainty startled her, more so because she couldn't think why he didn't want to let her go ashore. During the last hour of their sail back to the island, she thought and thought, but she couldn't come up with a logical reason to explain his action.

# CHAPTER FIVE

SAMANTHA FINGERED the stem of her wine glass. A few drops of red wine colored the bottom. The scarlet spectacular of sunset made no impression on her as it faded into a purpling twilight. Nothing had since she had become preoccupied with the question that remained unanswered. Why hadn't Chris wanted her to leave the boat?

Her gaze slid to him and found him studying her. She smiled quickly and took her hand away from the empty glass, realizing that neither of them had spoken for the past several minutes. The tip of her tongue nervously moistened her lower lip as she searched for an innocuous comment.

"It's peaceful, isn't it?" she said.

"Yes."

Both had changed for dinner that evening. He was wearing a white turtleneck shirt with a dark blue blazer and light blue slacks. This was another thing that confused Samantha. With all his money, she wondered why he didn't have jackets tailored to fit his broad shoulders and muscular chest. What he was wearing was attractive, but it would have been more so if it wasn't so tight around the shoulders.

Sighing, she rose from the table, smoothing her palms over the soft material covering her hips. The crimson two-piece suit had a floor-length culotte skirt and a long-sleeved top with the complementing draping folds of a tunic neckline. The vivid color accented the silky brown of her hair.

"Restless again?" Chris questioned, rising from the table, too.

"Again?" Her head jerked toward him, his question disconcerting her.

"Last night you couldn't sleep," he reminded her.

"Oh, yes," Samantha nodded her understanding. She supposed she hadn't done a very good job of concealing her abstraction. This was one time when she wasn't prepared to be candid, not until she had some hints of what was going on. Since he was prepared to blame her distraction on a restlessness, she was ready to go along with it. "I suppose I am a bit restless," she admitted.

"Rather than risk a repeat of last night, I think I should suggest a walk before midnight."

Samantha flipped the hair away from her cheek. "Not a bad idea." But her voice was hollow.

As they stepped through the patio door into the dusk, Chris glanced around. "Did you want to just walk or do you have a particular destination in mind?"

After an indecisive movement, she answered, "The gazebo."

His hand lightly rested on the back of her waist, and she let the slight pressure guide her toward the path she had taken the previous night. A scattering of pine needles littered the path, rustling under the soles of her sandals. Samantha couldn't ignore her awareness of the footsteps accompanying her, nor the invading warmth of his hand on her lower spine.

It had been a mistake to come out here, she decided, but it was too late to turn back now. The lengthening shadows of the trees seemed to shut out the rest of the world. It was a relief when they thinned and the gazebo was before her. She breathed easier as Chris's hand fell away, her pulse reverting to a less erratic beat.

Walking onto the octagonal platform, she paused on the side closest to the river. The smooth surface of the water was shimmering with the approaching darkness, reflecting the dying light of the sunset. Chris stood next to her, a shoulder leaning against a post, a leg bent to rest his foot on the wooden seat, but his attention wasn't fixed on the river. He was watching her with alertness veiled by aloof indolence.

"Is something troubling you, Sam?" he asked quietly after several minutes of silence had passed.

"What makes you ask that?" she returned lightly as if the question was really quite ridiculous.

But her gaze could only make a pretense of meeting the penetration of his. Mostly it skittered over the rugged masculinity of his features.

"You look as if you have something on your mind." The thread of seriousness didn't leave his tone despite her attempt to jest.

"Doesn't everybody?" Samantha shrugged, trying

to indicate to him that it really wasn't important.

She found it difficult to think with him so nearby. It became worse when he straightened as if he wanted a closer look at her expression.

Pretending an indifference that her thudding heart was far from endorsing, Samantha tipped back her head to gaze at the sky shading into a midnight blue. The first evening star winked at her and the silver crescent of the moon occupied another corner of the sky. The setting was too disturbingly romantic for her peace of mind. The musky scent of his after-shave cologne drifted in the air, and a sigh broke unwillingly from her lips.

"Did you enjoy yourself today?"

"Oh, yes." Her head turned jerkily to face him, an artificial smile of enthusiasm curving her lips. "The islands are lovely."

A breeze from the river teased at her hair, blowing a few strands across her cheek to be caught in the moist corner of her mouth. She lifted her hand to brush them away, but his fingers were already there pushing the silky strands behind her ear, then tangling his fingers in the thickness of the hair at the back of her neck.

At almost the same moment, he slid his other hand under her arm and around her back, drawing her to the right side of his chest. Startled, she gripped the flexing muscles of his right arm, pressing the heel of her other hand against his left shoulder to arch away from him.

But the enigmatic darkness of his compelling gaze

held her captive. She should protest, but she didn't really want to. He had to be aware of that fact. He was too experienced not to know when a woman wanted to be kissed. He let several more seconds stretch tautly to heighten her anticipation.

Then his mouth settled warmly over hers, caressing and arousing and melting the stiffness of her lips. Samantha had neither the will nor the desire to withstand his persuasive expertise. Her limbs weakened under the sensual assault until she was leaning against his hard length for support.

This response brought an insistent demand to his kiss, parting her lips, the invasion and possession more vividly exhilarating than any sensation she had ever known. The taste of his mouth was an aphrodisiac, heady and addictive. Her hips were molded against the solid muscles of his thighs.

In the sweetness of surrender, her fingers clung to his arm, the half fist of her right hand spreading open to caress the bulge of his shoulder. He caught her right wrist, lifting his head to gaze into the dazed shimmer of her eyes. The smoldering darkness of his charcoal eyes revealed the physical disturbance her response had made on him, although he was more in control of his emotions than she was.

For several seconds the iron band of his muscular arm continued to press her against his length while he held her wrist in his hands. A thumb rubbed the sensitive inside of her wrist while her pulse was drumming.

The line of his jaw tightened in decision. Samantha

was set away from him as he turned, moving into the shadows. Light flared and a match flame was cupped to a cigarette. In the next instant, a lit cigarette was thrust into her hand.

She accepted it shakily, inhaling on the filtered tip and hoping the nicotine would have the desired calming effect. But the silence was unnerving. She had certainly made it obvious that she had enjoyed his kiss and hadn't indicated any desire for it to end. So why had he ended the embrace?

There was a possible explanation, one that filled her with waves of self-disgust for reacting so naturally to his caresses. And the possible explanation made it necessary that she attempt to restore some of her pride.

"You weren't obliged to kiss me, Chris." Her voice was treacherously husky. She felt the thrust of his sharp gaze, but continued looking over the river. "When I agreed to your suggestion of a night walk, that was all I expected. It never occurred to me that the moonlight might make you think I was anticipating a flirtation."

"Is that why you think I kissed you?" There was a grim hardness in his voice. His fingers caught her chin, turning her face to the moonlight so he could view its expression. Her eyes had lost their dazed look and were wide and frank. "Out of a sense of duty because of the moonlight?"

"Isn't it?" Samantha countered, faintly accusing. "After all, I am your guest and Reuben Gentry's daughter."

"Therefore," he followed her train of thought aloud, "I'm entertaining you even to the point of indulging any romantic fantasies you might have about the magic of moonlight." The freezing scorn in his voice hinted at a savage fury. "You couldn't be farther from the truth, Miss Gentry, in nearly every respect."

"I don't understand." A confused frown partially arched an eyebrow as she searched the shadows to see his face.

"It isn't necessary you do." Clipped and harsh. "Nothing is necessary except—" Abruptly he checked the rest of the sentence, staring at her for taut seconds.

An expletive was muttered beneath his breath. Her chin was released and the cigarette torn from her grasp to be thrown into the night. An iron trap closed around her, pinning her arms tightly. A fiery passion was consuming her lips, whirling her into a vortex of sensations before she could assimilate what was happening. She yielded to the demands of his mouth, her lips parting under the brutal pressure of his, a savage sweetness in the pain he inflicted.

Her flesh pliantly allowed itself to be molded against the intimate contours of his masculine shape. Her hands, wanting to encircle his neck, had to be satisfied with spreading over his chest, fingers slipping inside the lapels of his jacket. Arching her farther backward, he abandoned the responsive delights of her mouth to scorch her face with kisses, then nibbling at her neck until a moaning sigh of pain and passion came from her throat. There was no support from her legs and his arms took her weight. Her hands searched for a way to cling to him, her fingers encountering smooth leather as they curled into the knit of his turtleneck.

He stiffened, then dragged himself away, capturing her hands and holding them against his chest. She could feel his ragged breathing as she swayed unsteadily toward him, not meaning to, but unable to stop. The narrowed screen of his dark lashes concealed the desire she knew had to be burning in his eyes. She guessed her own reflected it and lowered them from the penetrating scrutiny of his gaze. She stared instead at the large hands imprisoning hers.

"I must be out of my mind to get mixed up with you," he breathed savagely.

"I—" Samantha began.

"For God's sake, don't say any more!" he snapped angrily. "It's bad enough already! Come on." He jerked her to the side, his fingers bruising the tender flesh of her arm as he pushed her toward the path, yet keeping her close enough to him that she felt his left shoulder brushing against hers. "We're going back to the house before this gets out of hand."

But it wasn't the harsh command of his voice that stopped Samantha from protesting. It was the fleeting touch of something hard against her shoulder and a series of memories that suddenly joined together like pieces of a puzzle.

The poorly tailored jackets and the fact that she had seen him only once when he wasn't wearing a jacket of sorts. The way he had abruptly ended both embraces when she had started to hold him. The leather she had touched under his jacket. The hard, inanimate object that had just brushed her shoulder.

And most of all, the memory of the previous night when she thought she had seen him slip a gun inside his windbreaker. She hadn't thought she'd seen it—she had. What was more, he was wearing a shoulder holster now.

Why? Why was he wearing it? For protection against the possibility of intruders? No, Samantha couldn't accept that; the threat was't that great. *Ask him*, an inner voice prodded. Laugh and tease him that he found her so dangerous he carried a gun. But the cold waves of fear she was experiencing froze her into silence.

They were nearing the house, its lights growing brighter. She stumbled and the grip on her arm tightened cruelly to steady her, and she bit her lip to keep back the cry of pain. Her arm wasn't released until they were a few steps from the door.

As she entered the house, Samantha tried to keep a few feet advantage, moving awkwardly into the empty living room. She stood uncertainly near the massive stone fireplace, unable to escape any farther. He stopped just inside the room and she felt the hooded scrutiny of his look.

Keeping her back to him, she forced her twisting hands apart and raked her fingers through her hair. Her heart pounded as loudly as a hammer in the pregnant silence. If only he would stop studying her as if she were a slide under a microscope, she thought desperately. The width of the room separated them, yet she could think no more clearly now than when she had been in his arms.

"I'll have Maggie bring us some coffee," he announced abruptly, irritation making his voice tight and faintly harsh.

"No." Samantha swung around, breathing in sharply as she became impaled by his rapier gaze. Although an unknown terror was racing her pulse, the sudden tremors that quaked through her were caused by his overpowering virility. "I don't care for any coffee," she declared after a second's pause. "I...I didn't get much sleep last night. I think I'll make an early night of it."

With the decision made, she started toward the corridor leading to her bedroom. She glimpsed a movement from him and wanted to bolt, but she forced herself, her feet, not to hurry.

"Sam!" his voice commanded slowly.

In the hall opening, she stopped, trying to meet his slate gray eyes without betraying her inner trepidation. As slow, seemingly lazy strides brought him closer, she felt her knees weakening and rested a hand against the wall for support.

Chris halted a foot away, bronzed, rawboned features gazing down at her, lean and hard, rugged and compelling. The line of his mouth had thinned in grimness. His jaw was clenched and taut.

His hand reached out to touch her cheek, his thumb lightly rubbing her smooth skin. Samantha trembled visibly, as his caress flamed through her. Quickly she lowered her gaze, but avoided looking at the bulge on the left side of his blazer. Not even fear could check the desire to be in his arms.

"Please, I'm tired." She tried to speak with bright unconcern.

His thumb slipped under her chin to tilt it upward. "Sam, I . . . ." The urgency of his low voice never had an opportunity to convey its message.

Footsteps approached the living room and his hand fell away as he turned to meet them. Granted a reprieve, Samantha took advantage of it.

"Good night, Chris," she murmured as Tom appeared in the living room. She hurried down the corridor to her bedroom.

Within minutes she was in bed with the lights out. She lay awake for long hours in the dark, thinking. Each time she tried to concentrate on his possible reasons for carrying a gun, her thoughts kept turning to the way he had kissed her and the undiluted passion he had aroused in her.

It didn't make for a restful sleep when she finally did doze. But it was a light sleep that had her rising before eight the next morning.

Chris was already breakfasting when she entered the dining room. His detached greeting was unexpected. Samantha assumed a similar attitude, especially after she noticed the bulge on his left side under the tan bush jacket. Orange juice, coffee and toast were on the table. Her appetite didn't stretch to more than that and she refused Maggie's offer of bacon and eggs when the woman appeared briefly in the room.

"Was there anything you needed from town?" The question was offered negligently as Chris lit a cigarette.

Samantha stared at the slice of half-eaten toast in her hand. After his suspicions yesterday, the inquiry was a surprise. He seemed to be suggesting a shopping expedition. Everything imaginable had been awaiting her arrival here and she couldn't think of a thing that had been overlooked. She wasn't going to admit that, though.

"There are a couple of things," she lied smoothly and let her teeth crunch off a bite of toast.

"Make a list and give it to Maggie. She'll see that you get whatever you need." He shook out the match and tossed it into an ashtray.

Her gaze sliced across the table to his bland expression of aloofness. So she wasn't to be allowed to go into town. But she had to make certain that was really what he meant and it wasn't just her imagination.

"That isn't necessary," she denied, smiling falsely as she added a spoonful of marmalade to her toast. "I'll ride along with her to town. It'll be fun wandering through the shops."

"Maggie isn't going to town." His cryptic reply forced Samantha to meet the hooded charcoal of his gaze. Coiled and alert behind that masked look of ease, he held her attention.

"I don't understand," Samantha laughed self-consciously.

"She's ordering by phone what supplies we need

and a launch will bring them out this afternoon," he explained.

"Oh." A small voice of understanding.

There was nothing left to say and she began munching on the marmalade-covered toast. Its sweetness was suddenly cloying.

The morning hours dragged. It was an effort to appear natural and not be consumed by all the suspicions and doubts that had surfaced. And, after last night's tempestuous kisses, Chris's withdrawn behavior was disturbing. He avoided any opportunity to touch her, however innocent the reason, and Samantha's awareness of him was heightened to a fever pitch. The air around her crackled as if an electrical storm was approaching.

Surreptitiously, she glanced at Chris. He was lounging in one of the patio chairs, seemingly unaffected by the undercurrents tormenting her. From where Samantha leaned in a half-sitting position against a protruding rock, his craggy profile was offered for her inspection. Masculine with his sun-bronzed vitality, he appeared relaxed, the tapering length of him stretched out. The even rise and fall of his chest suggested sleep.

They had gone out to the patio after lunch, a meal that Samantha barely tasted, her nerves too overwrought. Her bearing was tuned for the sound of a motorboat, which was the only reason she had agreed to come out on the patio.

Several had passed, catching her interest at the first sound and losing it when they continued by the island. The dull hum of another boat was approaching and she tensed as it droned increasingly louder. Then came the sound she had been waiting to hear. The boat's engine was throttled down.

With another glance at Chris, Samantha straightened warily from the rock, not certain whether he was sleeping or had merely closed his eyes. Striving for nonchalance, she stuffed her fingertips in her denim pockets and strolled quietly toward the path leading to the boathouse where the supply launch would dock.

"Going for a walk?" The lazy voice paralyzed her for an instant.

She turned jerkily toward his chair. "I thought I might." Her smile was tight.

"Headed anywhere in particular?" Behind the idle question she sensed a sharpness.

She hesitated. Should she answer truthfully or lie? No, it had to be the truth. She needed to know exactly what her position was. Her imagination was working overtime. She had to know if what she was thinking was true. Inwardly she was trembling from the decision and its possible consequences.

"I thought I'd walk to the cove," she replied and noted the flicker of grimness around his mouth. While she still had the courage, she plunged forward. "The launch with the supplies is docking now. I heard it a few minutes ago."

"That's hardly an event," he mocked dryly.

"No, but I'm going just the same. Any objections?" She couldn't keep from challenging him even though her heart was in her throat.

"Not really," he answered, but every instinct said that he was lying. He rolled leisurely to his feet. "Do you mind if I make a more stimulating suggestion? Since you want to go to the cove, why not change into your swimsuit first, then we could swim for a couple of hours?"

It seemed a simple suggestion, but Samantha recognized his stalling tactics.

"By the time I changed, the launch would be gone," she pointed out.

"Does it matter?" His hands had slid to his hips, his stance arrogant, the quietness of his voice intimidating.

"Since I was going to the cove to meet the boat, yes, it does matter," she retorted, tipping her head to the side, openly defiant. "But maybe you don't want me to meet the launch? That's why you're trying to think up ways to stop me, isn't it?"

"Now that's foolish." The smile he flashed was cold and without humor.

"Is it?" Samantha taunted. "I don't think so."

"Come on, Sam." He frowned at her words and shook his head. "Why would I want to do a thing like that?"

Pivoting, she stalked toward the path, angered that she had let herself be manipulated that way. He had a streak of cunning as well as ruthlessness. The sound of firm, striding steps on the path behind her chased away the anger.

Looking over her shoulder, Samantha's widened eyes saw him lessening the distance between them.

Since he hadn't been able to stop her through guile, she guessed he wouldn't be above using force.

She bolted from the path into the trees and thick undergrowth and heard Chris call her name, angered and impatient, but this only spurred her on. Branches whipped at her arms and legs as she ran blindly, trying to make a straight line to the cove where the old path had curved. Above her own noise, she could hear the rustle of brush behind her. He was chasing her, but she didn't dare risk a glance back.

There was a small clearing ahead and she ran for it, aware of the noise coming closer. Breaking free of the brush and trees, she tried to dash across the clearing and regain some of the lead she had lost, when a large hand grabbed her arm just below the elbow, pulling her up short and spinning her around.

Her forward impetus deprived her of balance. She couldn't change direction that abruptly and maintain her footing. She tumbled to the ground, dragging him to his knees as she fell. A thick cushion of pine needles broke her fall, pungent and dried by the sun.

Instantly she was kicking and twisting to get to her feet. She nearly made it, but a muscular arm flung her back to the ground. She struck out at him, swinging her fists at any part of him she could hit, attacking him with all the viciousness of a trapped animal. He soon captured her flailing arms and stretched them spread-eagled above her head.

Samantha struggled all the more violently, breathing in panicked sobs. Twisting and writhing, she tried to free herself of the weight pressing into the ground

# NO RISK, NO OBLIGATION TO BUY…NOW OR EVER!

## GUARANTEED

## PLAY "ROLL A DOUBLE" AND GET AS MANY AS FIVE GIFTS!

# HERE'S HOW TO PLAY:

1. Peel off label from front cover. Place it in space provided at right. With a coin, carefully scratch off the silver dice. This makes you eligible to receive two or more free books, and possibly another gift, depending on what is revealed beneath the scratch-off area.

2. You'll receive brand-new Harlequin Presents® novels. When you return this card, we'll rush you the books and gift you qualify for ABSOLUTELY FREE!

3. Then, if we don't hear from you, every month, we'll send you 6 additional novels to read and enjoy. You can return them and owe nothing, but if you decide to keep them, you'll pay only $2.49 per book—a saving of 40¢ each off the cover price.

4. When you subscribe to the Harlequin Reader Service®, you'll also get our newsletter, as well as additional free gifts from time to time.

5. You must be completely satisfied. You may cancel at any time simply by sending us a note or a shipping statement marked ''cancel'' or by returning any shipment to us at our expense.

The Austrian crystal sparkles like a diamond! And it's carefully set in a romantic "Key to Your Heart" pendant on a generous 18" chain. The entire necklace is yours free as added thanks for giving our Reader Service a try!

DETACH AND MAIL CARD TODAY!

# HARLEQUIN "NO RISK" GUARANTEE

- You're not required to buy a single book—ever!
- You must be completely satisfied or you may cancel at any time simply by sending us a note or shipping statement marked "cancel" or by returning any shipment to us at our cost. Either way, you will receive no more books; you'll have no obligation to buy.
- The free books and gift you claimed on this "Roll A Double" offer remain yours to keep no matter what you decide.

If offer card is missing, please write to: Harlequin Reader Service, 3010 Walden Ave., P.O. Box 1867, Buffalo, NY 14269-1867

BUSINESS REPLY MAIL

FIRST CLASS MAIL    PERMIT NO. 717    BUFFALO, NY

POSTAGE WILL BE PAID BY ADDRESSEE

HARLEQUIN READER SERVICE
3010 WALDEN AVE
PO BOX 1867
BUFFALO NY 14240-9952

NO POSTAGE
NECESSARY
IF MAILED
IN THE
UNITED STATES

DETACH AND MAIL CARD TODAY!

as he half straddled and half lay on top of her. Her head moved from side to side in desperate effort, tangling her brown-silk hair in its pillow of pine needles. He held her easily, letting her struggle uselessly until her energy was spent.

Finally, gasping, Samantha had no more strength left to fight. She glared resentfully into the smoldering steel of his eyes, her heart thudding against her ribs from her exertions. The pine needles were brushing roughly against the bare skin of her arms. She was crushed under his weight, the heat from his body nearly burning the entire length of her.

The hard muscles of his thighs pressed down on her legs. Her breasts were nearly flattened by the granite wall of his chest. Steel-hard fingers gripped the wrists she no longer strained to break free. Mixing with the pine scent was the musky fragrance of his maleness heightened by perspiration to an intoxicating level.

The frustration of defeat gradually gave way to an awareness of the dangerous intimacy of her position. As the knowledge flickered in her rounded brown eyes, she saw it reflected in his. She was afraid to move, afraid if she did, it would be to invite the possession of his kiss.

Tension mounted, her gaze locked by the magnetic force of his. When his charcoal gaze slid to her lips, they softened under its nearly physical caress.

Slowly, taking his time, his mouth descended toward hers, and Samantha exhaled a sighing surrender. Flames were kindled by the languid passion of his kiss, arousing her desire more swiftly than demanding possession would have done. Expertly he explored every corner of her lips and mouth until she quivered boneless in response.

Her arms were released and she wound them around his neck and shoulders. The crushing weight of his body pressing down on her added fuel to the fire raging through her veins, a wild song ringing in her heart. The intimate caress of his hands was an erotic stimulant that brought an urgency to her response. Immediately his kiss hardened in a complete mastery of her senses.

Every nerve end was attuned to him, quivering at his touch. His fingers tugged at the buttons of her blouse, unfastening to gain access to the rounded flesh the material had concealed. As he pushed the strap from her shoulder to release the last confinement, he dragged his mouth away from her lips to plunder the sensitive skin of her throat and shoulders with rough kisses, blazing a fiery trail to the swelling peak of her breast. The sensual touch of his tongue drew a shuddering moan from her throat. His hard male need made her aware of the empty throbbing of her loins and their mindless plea for satisfaction.

His hand remained to cup her breast as he raised his lips toward her mouth, checking his movement tantalizing inches from his goal to read the message in the liquid brown of her eyes.

The gray smoke of his eyes flamed possessively over her face.

An inch from his lips, Samantha knew that this time his kiss would demand an ultimate surrender. She was beyond the point of resisting. She could deny him nothing. The flames of love encircling her heart had vanquished everything else but her wish to be his.

But he stiffened. A sudden alertness entered the dark gray of his eyes as his gaze warily swerved away from her face. Bewildered for a second, Samantha finally heard the sound of someone walking heavily, nearing the spot where they lay entwined on the pine-needle bed.

She breathed in sharply, a combination of alarm, embarrassment and protest. Before she could exhale, Chris's large hand was clamped over her mouth, his piercing gaze warning her into silence.

# CHAPTER SIX

IT SEEMED an eternity before the footsteps drew level with their position, receded into the silence of the woods, and the hand was removed from its smothering hold over her mouth. The footsteps had passed within a few feet of them, the thick underbrush screening them from the trail running from the cove to the house.

Soundlessly Chris rolled to his feet and gazed in the direction of the house. Samantha wasn't nearly as quiet as she scrambled to her feet. There had been time to consider the wisdom of her actions and find there was none. She had been ready to give herself to a man who was virtually keeping her a prisoner on this island. She had nearly made his power over her unlimited.

Her fingers fumbled with the buttons of her blouse. They were still shaking too severely from the devastation of his lovemaking to accomplish their task. Her gaze was directed at their ineffectual movements, but she was aware of him moving to stand in front of her. She was incapable of looking at him.

"Sam." The caressive warmth of his voice flowed over her.

When she refused to look at him, his fingers captured her hands and pulled them away from her blouse, permitting it to gape open. He made a thorough inspection of her feminine attributes, his gaze seeming to strip away the lacy bra. Still holding her hands, he twisted them gently behind her back and drew her hips against his muscular thighs. Her bones felt like putty in his hands.

"No!" Desperately Samantha denied the turmoil caused by his nearness.

"No?" His voice was low and mocking, his breath warm against her skin.

"No," she repeated, more decisively this time as she lifted her gaze to his face. The dark glow of his gray eyes nearly destroyed her will to resist. "You wanted me to miss the launch," she accused, "and you've succeeded. Now let me go."

His gaze narrowed to pinpoints of sharp steel. The muscles along his strong jawline worked for convulsive seconds before he released her and stepped away, his expression hard and withdrawn.

Turning her back to him, Samantha quickly fastened the buttons of her blouse with none of the fumbling ineptitude of before. Without another glance in his direction, she started toward the thick undergrowth that separated the little clearing from the trail.

"Where are you going?" His voice rumbled low and ominous in command.

"To the house," she flashed over her shoulder, sarcasm issuing to hide the pain. "Any objections?"

"None," he snapped coldly.

Samantha didn't stop until she had closed her bedroom door. She leaned weakly against its support, her legs trembling. The reflection in the mirror above the dresser revealed her dishevelled appearance, pine needles clinging to her hair and clothes. Pushing herself away from the door, she started walking toward the private bathroom, stripping off the soiled garments as she moved across the room.

Without waiting for the water to adjust to a comfortable temperature, she stepped beneath the freezing shower spray. But the stinging needles couldn't erase the memory of the intimate touch of his hands, nor could the cold water chill the warmth lingering from the fires he had kindled.

Finally, she turned off the taps in defeat, wrapped one towel around her wet hair and with another covered her nakedness. With robotlike movements she returned to the bedroom, pulling clean undergarments from the dresser drawer and walking to the closet. She tossed a pair of light bue bell-bottoms onto the bed and reached for the matching pin-striped blouse.

With it in her hand, she noticed the blue windbreaker she had borrowed from Chris the night she had arrived. She wanted no physical reminders of him. Her fingers gripped the smooth material to violently jerk it from its hanger. It was halfway off the hanger when her arm became paralyzed, unable to complete the movement.

In numbed disbelief, she stared at the inside collar of the jacket. Black lettering spelled out the initials

C.S. That was all, just C.S. Not C.S.A. for Christopher Steven Andrews. Slowly she pulled it from the hanger, examining closely to see if the last letter hadn't somehow become faded. It didn't taken an expert to discern that there never had been another letter following the S.

Crumpling the windbreaker in her hands, she turned to move to the bed. She sagged onto the edge, staring sightlessly at the jacket. One piece of incriminating evidence didn't prove the case. Too many times during the past few days she had been ready to accept the first information as the whole truth. She would not jump to conclusions again, not until she found something more to substantiate her discovery.

Not wanting to risk losing what she had, she stuffed the windbreaker between the mattress and box springs of the bed. The towel around her middle was cast aside as she hurriedly dressed in the clean clothes. Rubbing the worst of the dampness from her hair, she ran a quick comb through it and called it good enough. Entering the hallway, she closed the door on the cyclone mess of dirty clothes and wet towels strewn about the room. Tidying up could wait. Right now there was only one thought in her mind. The living room was empty and she breathed a sigh of relief and satisfaction.

With a cautious glance toward the adjoining rooms, she moved quietly to the study corner, her gaze seeking and finding the briefcase leaning against the side of the desk. She knelt beside it, pushing a clinging strand of hair from her cheek.

Her palms were wet with nervous perspiration, and she wiped them on the material of her slacks before reaching for the briefcase, keeping it upright to examine the area near the handle. The gold initials C.S. looked boldly back at her.

Minutely Samantha examined the leather for any mark or scar that would indicate a third letter had once been there. It never had. She had wanted proof to substantiate the markings on the windbreaker and she had found it. She slid the briefcase back to its former position, her hands settling on her knees to push herself upright.

"What are you doing?" The low, accusing male voice sent shafts of cold fear plunging into her heart.

Samantha turned her head slowly toward Chris standing in the archway to the dining room, his immobility a challenging threat. But he wasn't Chris. Whoever he was, he wasn't Chris Andrews—nor Owen Bradley. Nervously she moistened her lips and straightened. Should she confront him with her discovery? No, she decided, not until she had a chance to think it over.

Her mind raced to find a plausible explanation for why she had been kneeling beside the desk. There wasn't any. Her only hope was to bluff her way out.

"It's none of your business what I was doing." With head held high, she started toward the hallway.

But his long strides caught her before she could reach it. Her wrist was brutally seized and twisted to jerk her toward him. The raging anger of his gaze scorched her face.

"I asked you a question and I want an answer," he growled threateningly.

The pain from his grip was excruciating. The slightest additional pressure would snap the delicate bones in her wrist. Samantha gritted her teeth against the physical agony slicing through her arm, but it helped her remain indifferent to the hard thrust of his thighs that she was forced to arch against.

Frigidly she glared at his harsh features. "Let go of me!" Each word was spoken with icy clarity. "I don't have to answer your question, and if you break my arm, you'll have to take me off the island to have it set."

He compressed his mouth into a taut line of checked violence. Samantha was released with an angry push before he pivoted to stride from the room. Weakly, she stared after him, feeling not at all victorious.

For the rest of the afternoon, she didn't budge from her room. Confusion muddled her thinking. She was obviously a prisoner. It didn't seem to matter whether the island, or her bedroom, formed her walls. The reason she was being held escaped her, no matter how many times she went over it.

If it hadn't been for the fact that she had spoken to her father and knew he was cognizant of her whereabouts, Samantha might have concluded that she had been kidnapped.

But Reuben did know.

The shadows outside had lengthened into evening hours when there was a knock on her door. She tensed, turning from the window to stare at the door.

"Who is it?" she demanded, knowing the answer before it was given.

"Chris," he answered, and opened the door.

*"Liar!* She wanted to scream at him. *You aren't Chris Andrews! I don't know who you are, but you are not Chris Andrews!* She glared at the bronze mask that so completely concealed any expression. But it wasn't the words on the tip of her tongue that she uttered.

"What do you want?" she asked coldly.

"Dinner's ready."

"Just send some bread and water to my room. That's good enough," she declared with taunting disdain.

The mask hardened. "You will come to the table and eat," he stated, then added, "if I have to drag you there and shovel the food down your throat."

Her gaze challenged the gray shards of his for a few more seconds before she submitted to his edict. The food was tasteless, but she ate some of it. She was aware every second of the speculating glances given her by Maggie and Tom.

Her tight-lipped silence wasn't something they could not notice. The instant dinner was over, she excused herself and retreated to her room, half expecting Chris—or whoever he was—to appear and order her into the living room. He didn't.

The next morning the prospect of spending the day in her bedroom wasn't at all appealing. If she was actually a prisoner, as it seemed she was, then there was no reason for her to be a willing prisoner. Besides, if there was more enlightening information to be obtained, it was unlikely she would learn it in the bedroom.

There was a determined light in her eyes as she emerged from her room. The germ of an idea was taking shape to confront her captor with the knowledge that she knew he was not Chris Andrews. Once he realized that she had seen through his guise, he might unwittingly provide her with some more information. The possibility put a spring to her step.

Rounding the arch into the living room, Samantha instantly spied the man seated at the desk, listening with glowering anger to the telephone at his ear. She stopped, alert to the violent impatience emanating from him. Whatever the person on the other end of the wire was saying, it was displeasing him greatly.

"Dammit, Reuben Gentry!" His voice rumbled across the room, widening Samantha's eyes. "Don't ever say I didn't warn you. You'll be sorry, very sorry." There was a pause, then, "You'll be hearing from me."

On that ominous note, he slammed the receiver and rose from the chair, leashed anger evident in the uncoiling swiftness of his movements. Samantha swallowed, and swallowed again when the lightning fury of his gaze jolted to her. His nostrils flared slightly, as if scenting danger. She couldn't deny overhearing the conversation. The best she could do was pretend she hadn't caught the promise of revenge.

"Was that my father?" she asked, somehow succeeding in hiding the tremors of fear.

"Yes."

Trying to maintain her pose of ignorance, Samantha strolled into the room. Her hands were trembling and she hooked her thumbs in the belt loops of her tight denims.

"When is he coming?" She tried to put just the right note of interest in her voice.

"He's... been delayed for a couple more days."

Samantha hadn't missed the infinitesimal pause in his answer. The penetrating gaze was difficult to meet, so she didn't try and turned instead toward the dining room.

Knowing she had to make some reply to his answer, she sighed ruefully. "I'm going to be back to work before Reuben ever succeeds in getting away." She quickly changed the subject. "Mmm, the coffee smells good this morning."

He allowed the conversation to be diverted, but Samantha wasn't certain she had fooled him. After hearing the telephone conversation, she didn't confront him with the knowledge that she knew he wasn't Chris Andrews.

It was slowly dawning on her that she just might be kidnapped. She had only his word that Reuben knew where she was.

In her mind, Samantha reran the short telephone conversation she had had with her father shortly after she had arrived on the island. First he had asked how she was, received her assurances that she was surviving (Samantha blanched at her choice of words in retrospect), then had tried to apologize for the delay.

But she had interrupted him before he explained the delay.

She had glossed over his apology with the assertion that she knew he was doing everything he could. And there had been his blankness when she had referred to Chris. Finally Reuben had admonished her to do whatever Chris told her. And couldn't her father's preoccupied air have been caused by concern for her safety?

Nausea gripped her stomach at the way the pieces to the puzzle fitted so perfectly. Unwittingly she had probably interrupted a telephone call demanding ransom. By speaking to Reuben, she had proved to him that they were truly holding her captive. If at any time she had betrayed an ignorance of her status or had started to indicate her whereabouts, Chris had been right there, listening to every word, ready to rip the phone away at the slightest provocation.

How easy she had made it for them, Samantha thought dejectedly. The mere mention of her father's name had persuaded her to come away with a perfect stranger. Not once had she questioned his credentials at the newspaper office. Beth had warned her to beware of him, but she hadn't listened. Not Samantha Gentry—she knew it all.

The newspaper office! Another memory staggered her. The letter that had been left for Harry Lindsey had to have been a ransom note. And she had pointed out which office to leave it in. It was all so sickeningly obvious now, even to the new clothes that had been provided for her. She hadn't been allowed to pack her

own things because of the risk of being seen with
Chris by more people and the delay it would have
caused in leaving.

The drive here to Clayton, New York, the fast car
that probably could have outdistanced any pursuer,
his preoccupation at the restaurant constantly watching everyone coming in and out, the man waiting to
take the car when they arrived and the young girl who
had joined him at the corner and who would undoubtedly resemble Samantha at a distance, the boat waiting a few minutes out. It all made so much sense now.

If Beth or anyone had happened to see her leave in
the car, the man and woman had probably driven it
miles away from there before ditching it. And there
hadn't been a soul around the dock to see Samantha
board the boat. She had even been ordered to wait in
the shadows of a building until it had docked, then
been sent below once on board. She had been a most
cooperative kidnap victim.

The island was an ideal place to hold her. There
weren't any nosy neighbors to see her or that she
could run to if she discovered what was happening.
The river provided the walls to keep her captive. The
boat tour of the islands had been to keep her entertained and not become suspicious of what was truly
going on. They hadn't stopped anywhere because
they didn't want to risk her being recognized. Possibly
her picture was in the papers. The same supposition
held true for the supply launch. Plus the fact that the
island was only a stone's throw from Canada and they
could slip across the border to escape once the ransom

had been paid. The ransom. The telephone call she had just overheard.

Fear took a stranglehold on her throat. Had Reuben refused to pay the ransom? Oh, God, it was possible, she thought. She had once heard him remark that if no ransoms were paid, there might not be any more kidnappings, declaring it was a crime of barbaric cruelty. Or had he been bluffing to gain time, taking a chance that the authorities, which she knew he would have called in, might find her?

Chris—or whatever his name was—had said "You'll be hearing from me." He could have meant that he would be calling back about the ransom or that he would be sending a message via her dead body. They couldn't very well let her go free, not when she could recognize them.

Her hands trembled and she quickly set the coffee mug on the table before she dropped it. Her gaze slid warily to the man seated across from her, only to drop to the table when she saw his inscrutable charcoal eyes watching her. How much of what she had been thinking had she revealed to him, she wondered in breathless panic.

"Are you all right? You look a bit peaked," he observed smoothly.

"A headache—migraine," Samantha lied glibly. "I'm prone to them the same as Reuben is." She touched shaking fingers to her temple and smiled wanly. "Excuse me, I think I'll go to my room and lie down for a while."

"Can I get you anything?" He didn't seem entirely

convinced, the faint quirk of his brow dryly mocking.

"No, thanks, she replied, quickly making her exit before he could probe further.

Restlessly Samantha paced the room for nearly an hour. She tried to consider the situation rationally and ignore the terror lurking in the corners of her mind. Although the stranger, her abductor—she had stopped thinking of him as Chris, the name didn't really fit him anyway—might be aware she suspected something funny was going on, he might not believe she had realized she was kidnapped. He probably still thought she was convinced he was Chris Andrews.

As his guest, she had to be permitted a certain latitude, though at the same time he was confident that she couldn't escape the island. The question was how could she take advantage of the limited freedom she did have on the island?

There had to be something she could do herself other than simply wait. She couldn't count on being released if the ransom was paid. Escape seemed impossible. Her only hope appeared to be being rescued. But how could she be rescued when no one knew where she was except the kidnappers?

A reporter was supposed to be resourceful, Samantha chided herself. There had to be some way she could get a message out without her abductors' knowledge. The supply launch would probably not come again, so that was out. No passersby ever stopped at the island, which ruled out the possibility of passing a message to them.

Of course, she thought wryly, there was always the

proverbial message stuffed in a bottle and tossed into the water, but the chance of anyone finding it in time would really be slim.

Frowning, she paused beside the window, staring out the panes at the green shadow of trees. What method of communication did that leave? The telephone! The clouds in her troubled brown eyes were dispelled by the light that suddenly brightened them.

Surely there was a way that she could persuade them to let her call her father for some innocent reason? Maybe during the conversation she could give Reuben a clue to where they were holding her. No, her cunning captor would see through the ruse and never permit any veiled message to be delivered.

Yet the telephone might still provide the means if she could use it without anyone listening in. That meant it had to be when no one was around. The middle of the night seemed an obvious choice, but Samantha discounted it. She remembered the night she had taken the midnight walk. No doubt someone was on watch all the time. Any night-time prowling stood a better chance of being discovered.

It had to be during the day when she was more or less free to roam the house and island at will. She would have to choose a time when all three of them were occupied. It was bold and brash, but infinitely more possible of success.

Footsteps sounded in the corridor outside her room. It could only mean someone was coming to check on her. Quickly Samantha flung herself on the bed, stretching out on her stomach and feigning sleep. Her heart was pounding like the roll of a snare drum as the door opened. Even though her eyes were closed, her senses recognized the identity of her intruder.

How many times in the past few days had his presence disturbed her sensually? Too many to count. Those mysteriously dark gray eyes were studying her now lying on the bed and she could feel the vague stirrings within. Samantha tried to breathe evenly, aware of his regard as surely as if he was touching her. Her stranger was dangerous in more ways than one.

When she thought she couldn't keep up the pretense of sleep any longer, she heard the door close. Still she didn't move, not immediately, not until she heard the quiet footsteps moving away from her door. Then she moved cautiously and began contemplating when she might stand the best chance of using the telephone.

At noon, it was Maggie who knocked on the door, coolly inquiring if Samantha would be having lunch. She maintained the excuse of a headache, hoping to lull them into not watching her so closely. When the housekeeper offered to bring her some broth, Samantha accepted, which maintained her pose of illness and provided nourishment for her empty stomach.

The door didn't latch securely behind Maggie. A few minutes after she had left the cup of beef broth, it slowly swung open a few inches, and from the living room, Samantha could hear the stranger's voice.

"I know she suspects something," he stated in a grim, decisive voice. "We couldn't hope to keep her completely in the dark. She's much too clever for that."

"But what are we going to do now?" came Tom's gruff response.

"Keep her on the island until...." The rest of his sentence became indistinct as they evidently moved to another room.

At least, Samantha smiled in macabre humor, there was no immediate plan to dispose of her. It would give her precious time to try to bring about her own rescue.

The opportunity presented itself much sooner than she expected. Almost an hour had passed when she heard the low murmur of voices outside, those of Tom and her stranger. At this time, Samantha knew, Maggie would be in the kitchen clearing away the luncheon dishes. This was her chance, maybe her only chance.

Stealthily, she tiptoed out of her room, down the corridor and into the living room. Listening intently she could hear Maggie in the kitchen and the faint voices outside. Adrenalin pumped through her veins as she picked up the telephone and hurriedly dialed her father's office number.

Her gaze darted apprehensively toward the kitchen as she waited for the telephone to be answered, winding a finger in the coiled cord. Exhilaration flashed through her when a woman's voice came through the receiver.

"Reuben Gentry, please," she requested in a whisper. "This is his daughter calling."

"I'm sorry, but I can barely hear you. Would you please speak up?" the woman insisted.

Samantha gritted her teeth impatiently. "I can't!" she hissed a little louder, silently cursing the wasted seconds. "This is Samantha Gentry, and I *must* talk to my father."

"Did you say it was Mr. Gentry you wanted?" The frowning voice asked for clarification.

"Yes!"

"I'm sorry, he isn't in right now. Can someone else help you?"

"Damn!" she muttered under her breath, rubbing a hand across her forehead. "Put me through to the security...."

The front doorknob was turning. She caught the movement out of the corner of her eye. Her stranger must be coming and she didn't stand a chance of getting out of the living room unseen. The odds were he would see her with the telephone in hand before she could replace it. Her only hope was to leave a message.

Precious time was wasted in making the decision. The door was already opened and the stranger walking in when Samantha turned her concentration to the receiver mouthpiece.

"Tell my father," she began in a loud, clear voice so the woman would have no trouble understanding what she said, "that I'm at—"

A large hand was pressing down the button on the telephone's cradle, breaking the connection before Samantha could complete her message. Frustration and impotent anger glared from her eyes as she looked into the pair of hard gray ones. He pried the receiver from the death-grip of her fingers and replaced it.

"I'm sorry," he said calmly, "I couldn't let you do that."

"You have no right to stop me!" Samantha flashed. "It was a private call. There was something I wanted to talk to Reuben about and I didn't have a chance to speak to him this morning," she defended herself with a lie. "I would have reimbursed you for the long-distance charges."

"I'm sure you would have." He towered beside her, an arm brushing her shoulder.

Inwardly Samantha was quaking, from fear and his disturbing nearness, but she boldly reached again for the telephone receiver. "Then there isn't any reason for you to object if I call him."

His hand clamped over her wrist, not allowing her to lift the receiver. "Sam, I'm not playing games," he warned quietly.

"Aren't you?" Her head jerked toward him, her brown eyes shimmering with defiance and rebellion. Temper threw caution to the winds. "You've been playing games with me ever since you walked into the newspaper office—first letting me believe you were Owen Bradley, then ly—" She bit into her lip, realizing she had virtually admitted that she knew he wasn't Chris Andrews.

The narrowing of his gaze indicated that he had guessed what she had been about to say. Her heart

skipped several beats under his piercing look. Samantha had gone too far to turn back. Her only hope was
to brave it out without revealing how terrified she
really was.

"I don't know who you are, but you aren't Chris
Andrews," she declared. "It was all a lie."

"More or less," he acknowledged with remorseless
ease.

Spinning away from him in irritation, Samantha
muttered, "I don't suppose it would do any good to
ask what your real name is?"

He hesitated. "My name is Jonas—"

"Jonas!" Laughing derisively in disbelief, she pivoted back. Her hand sliced the air to cut the rest of his
identification off. "Don't bother with the rest. That
isn't your name, either."

He slowly looked her up and down in a thoughtful
manner then shook his head in unconcern. "Names
aren't all that important."

"No," she agreed bitterly. "A man's character or
his lack of it remains the same regardless of his name.
Jonas is as good a choice as any. It's certainly appro-
priate. I haven't had anything but bad luck since I met
you."

"So you've decided I'm lacking in morals." There
was a glitter of harsh mockery in the eyes of the man
who now called himself Jonas.

"You've proved that!" she retaliated. "Just how
gullible do you think I am? How many times am I
supposed to believe your lies? You're keeping me a
prisoner on this island. You won't let me off and you

won't allow me to see anyone but you, Tom and Maggie. I'm not even permitted to phone my father. What story are you going to come up with to explain all that?''

"None." The rugged bronze features were hardening into glacial ice. "I don't think you would believe anything I tell you."

"You can't expect me to!" Samantha cried. A part of her had been wishing he would weave another believable story. She didn't want him to be a kidnapper. "You've cried wolf so many times that it's impossible! Oh, Chris—Jonas, whatever your name really is," she sighed impatiently, "why can't you let me leave a message for Reuben?"

She didn't know why she asked that. She knew he would never agree to it. The humbling plea had been a gesture of desperation and tears welled in her brown eyes.

His hands settled on her shoulders as he gazed deeply into her eyes, his jaw clenched. "I can't, Sam."

The force of his magnetism and her own attraction to it nearly pulled Samantha into his arms. Instead she wrenched her shoulders away from his grip, hating the way her traitorous heart refused to listen to her mind.

"It's not that you can't! You won't!" she accused in an emotion-choked voice.

"Think what you like," he replied grimly.

"Oh, don't worry, I will," Samantha assured him in a threatening tone.

She stood before him, her hands balled into fists at

her side, tears trembling on the ends of her lashes. This was not the way she had intended to confront him. She had planned to interrogate him merciless- ly, convicting him with the facts she already knew.

But somewhere along the way, she had stopped thinking of him as her captor and began looking at him as the man who had kissed her passionately and introduced her to feelings and sensations she hadn't known she possessed.

Beware of the stranger, she thought brokenly, be- cause he can steal your heart.

"I want your word, Sam, that you won't try to use the telephone again."

He regarded her steadily.

"My word?" she mocked. "Why should I give you my word?"

"Because if you don't, I'll be forced to cut the tele- phone line. I can't take the risk of your phoning any- one and letting them know you're here."

"Wouldn't it be easier just to lock me in my room?" Samantha challenged, her voice taut with misery.

"I hope it won't come to that." But his answer was a warning. "It's up to you."

Her freedom was limited, but she had to keep what little she had if she was going to have any chance at all to help herself.

"Very well, you have it." She had to give in and he had known it.

Pivoting on her heel, she voluntarily went to her room to think of another plan. A glance over her shoulder saw him standing in the same place watching her, his dark features hard and unyielding, and compellingly attractive.

# CHAPTER SEVEN

THE WATERS of the St. Lawrence were renowned for their fishing, with black bass and the battling muskie leading the list. Samantha had been watching the small fishing craft moving closer to the island for the past fifteen minutes. Its engine was put-putting in an erratic rhythm that suggested difficulties.

Stretched out on the raft anchored in the cove, she had toyed with the idea of swimming out to the boat. It was easily within her swimming range, but she knew she would not get ten feet before Jonas caught her. Glancing out of the corner of her eye, she saw he was watching the boat as intently as she was.

Since yesterday afternoon they had spoken little, exchanging only necessary remarks. He was her enemy, and Samantha couldn't allow her emotions to come into play.

The bow of the fishing boat swung to point toward the cove. Within seconds the sputtering motor died. His gaze sliced to her, a veiled warning in its narrowed gray depths, before it moved on to the stockily built man standing at the boathouse dock and watching the fishing boat.

"Find out what his trouble is, Tom," Jonas

ordered, his low voice carrying crisply across the dividing waters. "And get him out of here right away."

With a curt nod, Tom acknowledged the order. The fisherman stood up in his boat and waved toward shore. Jonas deliberately ignored the man's hailing. It was Tom who returned it before disappearing into the boathouse. A few minutes later he emerged, manning the oars of a dinghy, and rowed toward the disabled boat.

Propped by an elbow on her side, Samantha watched as Tom reached the boat, talked briefly with the man, then began rowing back. He never glanced toward the raft, but his voice was directed quietly to Jonas when he drew level with it.

"He ran out of gas."

A red gasoline can was in the dinghy when Tom started his second trip to the fishing boat. Frustration curled Samantha's fingernails into her palms. She could see her chance to contact someone from the outside world slipping away. She had to do something to get the fisherman's attention. There might not be another opportunity.

"Don't do anything foolish, Sam," his quiet steel voice warned.

Irritation snapped in her brown eyes at the way he had so perceptively guessed the direction of her thoughts. The wintry gray of his eyes didn't cool her determination. With lightning decision, she pressed her hands onto the raft boards to push herself upright, but she never completed the motion.

His reaction was swifter, rolling sideways from his sitting position to grip her shoulders and pin them to the hard wood decking. He loomed above her, muscular and bronze, a dark cloud of hairs curling virilely on his naked chest. The thumping of her heart had no basis in fear.

"Don't," he ordered. "Just keep quiet."

"You can't expect me to obey you," she hissed. "You know I have to try."

"Your screams won't mean anything. He'll think it's some joke," Jonas argued, a ruthless set to his hard features.

"He won't think it's a joke when I tell him who I am," Samantha retorted, and opened her mouth to scream.

His large hand closed over her jaw, holding it while he smothered her cry with the silencing force of his punishing kiss. The burning possession of his mouth flamed like wildfire through her veins, sweetly savage and torturously mad.

His demand for submission had her reeling light-headedly.

The full weight of his muscular body spread over her, its heat melting her bones. Although Samantha tried to resist, her toothpick defenses scattered seconds after he had claimed her lips. Pliant and responsive, she acceded to the urgent pressure of his kiss, completely forgetting that she was consorting with the enemy until she heard the reviving chug of the fishing boat's motor.

Samantha twisted free of the male lips in time to

see the fisherman wave to Tom and turn the boat in the opposite direction of the island, gathering speed as it left.

"No!" she moaned brokenly, staring at the boat's wake.

Jonas released her and levered himself away, leaving her flesh chilled where it had felt his warmth. Sickened by the way she had been unable to deny herself the heady pleasure of his kiss, she rested a hand across her eyes, as if shutting out the sight of him would hide the forbidden love she felt growing.

"Did you have to kiss me?" she hurled at him resentfully. "Or is it just a habit with you to maul your prisoners?"

"Believe me, if there'd been a more effective means to shut you up I would have used it." His tone was bitingly sardonic.

The stinging flick of his reply was just what Samantha needed to pull herself out of her misery. Rising to stand upright on trembling legs, she squarely met the wintry glitter of his gaze. Kissing him had been an ordeal for her, too, but one of an entirely different kind.

"In the future, please find another method," she declared, faintly haughty and very proud.

With animal grace he glided to his feet, the coiled alertness of a predator about him, the angry glint in his eye decidedly primitive. His superior height almost made Samantha feel dwarfed as he stood before her nearly naked, muscles rippling toast brown in the sun.

"Don't worry, Sam. I'll look for one," Jonas snapped.

"And don't call me Sam," she flashed. "That's reserved for people I like and trust!"

For several charged seconds the tension mounted as they glared at each other. The hard line of his mouth thinned ominously.

"It's time we went back to the house," he said finally.

"I'll bet you're sorry you didn't decide to lock me in my room," Samantha accused bitterly.

"I wouldn't bring it up if I were you. The idea is acquiring more merit every day," he warned.

She clamped her mouth shut. This was not the time to bait him or he might decide to carry out his threat. She had lost one opportunity to obtain help this afternoon. She would be a fool to throw away the chance to have more opportunities simply because she wanted to lash out and hurt him, trying to divert some of her pain to him. Swallowing her spiteful words, she turned and dived into the water. Jonas followed when she surfaced a few yards from the raft.

In the solitude of her room, Samantha relived the scene on the raft. The feeling of wretchedness returned at her failure to resist him and her failure to identify herself in some way to the fisherman. In the midst of her dejection came a glimmer of hope.

Escape from the island had always seemed impossible. The only means of transportation was by boat, and Samantha knew she would never be able to operate the sailboat. It was too large. Swimming to another island or the mainland was out because she had not the strength nor the endurance to cover the distance.

Today, another means of transportation had unknowingly been revealed to her. It was the dinghy that Tom had rowed to the fishing boat. One opportunity had been denied her and another had taken its place. It was up to her to make use of it.

The trick would be to leave without being seen. She not only had to get out of the house, but also make it to the boathouse and row away from the island unobserved. Broad daylight was ruled out. Supposing that she made it to the boat, there was the risk of her being seen on the river in the dinghy, and it would be too easy for Jonas to overtake her in the sailboat. If she was caught, Samantha had no doubt that she would be locked in her room after that.

Any attempt would have to be made in the middle of the night when the darkness could hide her, both on the island and on the water. She had slipped out once unseen, maybe she could succeed again. But this time she wouldn't walk boldly out of the door. Leaving the house would demand furtive action.

She walked to her bedroom window. The trees grew close to the house on this side of the building. There was only a narrow clearing that she would have to cross before reaching the concealing cover of the trees. From there she would have to work her way as quietly as possible to the boathouse path.

It would not be easy with all the thick undergrowth rustling beneath her feet and against her legs. And she would have to be careful not to lose her direction in the dark. A flashlight was out of the question to guide her footsteps.

The glass portion of the window would be raised, but the protective screen was a problem. It was secured from the outside, which meant Samantha would have to pry the wire screen free of its wooden frame. The only tools she had to use, if they could be called tools, were in her manicure set. It was a case of making do with what was at hand as she set to work on a loosened corner of the screen.

By the time she had an opening large enough to crawl through, she had only a few minutes to change out of the swimsuit that had dried on her and into some clothes for dinner. Excitement for her daring plan had built up. Suppressing it was difficult, but she couldn't risk Jonas suspecting her.

During the meal, she said little, letting Tom, Maggie and Jonas carry the conversation. She was aware of the frequency with which the gray eyes regarded her, and she could only hope that he interpreted her silence as being sullen. All the while she kept going over in her mind the route of her escape.

When Maggie began clearing the dishes from the table and Tom had left to look around outside, Samantha wished she could retreat to her room. But it was too soon, so she wandered into the living room.

"You don't have to keep me company," she informed Jonas acidly when he followed her into the living room. "There aren't any fishermen around."

He ignored her comment and lowered his tall frame

into a leather chair opposite the one Samantha had chosen. Trying to conceal her irritaion, she picked up a magazine and flipped indifferently through the pages.

"You've been very quiet tonight," he observed.

Samantha closed the magazine abruptly and tossed it on the side table. "Under the circumstances, you can hardly expect me to make scintillating conversation."

The line of his mouth curved, a movement totally lacking humor. "What scheme is running through your mind?"

"Scheme?" Although she tried to sound blank, Samantha realized the color had drained from her face, indicating the accuracy of his perception. She tried to conceal her escape plans in a false candor. "The only thing going through my mind right now is how can I get off this island prison of yours. And failing that, I'm trying to figure out how I can let others know where I am."

He shook a cigarette from his pack and offered it to her. She accepted, bending her head to the match flame in his hand. "Come up with any ideas?" Jonas inquired with the infuriating calm of a man confident that all possibilities had been covered.

Exhaling an impatient cloud of smoke, Samantha seized the first thought that occurred to her. "Yes, one."

"What's that?" A dark brow quirked mockingly in her direction.

"I've been considering burning the house down,"

she announced. "You have to admit that it isn't something that could be ignored. There would be people crawling all over this island within minutes of the first flame licking the roof."

"There would still be plenty of time for Tom and me to get you onto the sailboat and away from the island before the first person arrived," Jonas pointed out. "So it won't do you any good to play with matches."

"I know," sighed Samantha. For an instant, the spur of the moment idea had sounded possible.

"Surely you've had some other ideas," he prompted dryly.

"Well—" for the first time in several days, an impish gleam entered her eye as she remembered one of her more ridiculous thoughts "—I did consider getting a light and flashing a Morse code signal to any ships or boats going by the island."

"What stopped you?"

"I don't know Morse code," she answered ruefully. At his low chuckle, she regretted her lapse. It was hard enough to resist him without putting things on a lighter level. A grim resolve entered her voice when she spoke. "I'll think of something, though."

The cigarette was discarded, half-smoked, in the ashtray. The chair was too comfortable, inviting relaxation. Samantha pushed out of the chair, walking nervously to the fireplace, empty and blackened.

"Sam, I—" Jonas began quietly, a thread of solemnity running through his tone.

"I told you I don't want you to call me that." She

kept her back to him, looking sideways from her shoulder yet not allowing his craggy features to enter her vision. "The only thing I want from you is to leave this island."

"It isn't possible for you to leave. Not yet," he added stiffly.

"When?" demanded Samantha, doubting that he would ever let her leave.

He took a long time answering her and she turned slightly to see him. He was studying the smoke curling from the burning tip of his cigarette.

"When?" she repeated.

"I hope not much longer." His veiled look never left the cigarette.

What did he mean? Had arrangements been made by her father to pay the ransom? It seemed to be what his comment meant.

"Have you...have you talked to Reuben?" she asked, holding her breath.

"For a few minutes this afternoon," he admitted.

"What did he say?" she rushed.

His gaze flicked to her briefly, emotionless and aloof. "As I said before, it shouldn't be too much longer before you can leave here," he replied, not answering her question except in the most ambiguous terms.

"How long is not much longer?" Samantha persisted in her search for the time when the ransom was to be paid.

"Let's just leave it that it will be a little while yet," Jonas stated. "Then all this will be all over."

*And I'll never see you again.* The thought brought a sharp pain to the area of her heart. She turned away from him, knowing his image would haunt her for a long time. The mantel clock ticked in the silence for several minutes.

"I think I'll go to my room," she said finally. There was no point in staying there.

"Good night," Jonas offered when she stepped into the hall.

"Yes." Samantha hesitated. If everything went according to plan she would not see him again. Her gaze slid over him, masculine and vital. "Goodbye" hovered on the tip of her tongue. "Good night," was what she uttered.

There was not nearly the elation she had anticipated when she reached her room. She changed into her night clothes and laid out jeans and a dark blue pullover. Then she climbed into bed to wait for the house to become silent.

She knew there was no risk that she would fall asleep. There were too many things to think about and leaving Jonas was one of them. But that was the way it had to be. She simply couldn't trust him.

The luminous dial of the clock on her bedside table indicated the hour as one. There hadn't been a sound anywhere in the house for the past two hours. Samantha guessed that Tom was somewhere outside on watch since she hadn't heard anything to indicate his return. As she slid silently from beneath the covers, she crossed her fingers that he wasn't near the boathouse.

Dressed in the dark clothing that would help her to blend with the night's shadows, Samantha returned to the bed and stuffed the pillows beneath the covers to form the mock shape of a sleeping figure. The pale moonlight streaming through the window illuminated her handiwork without revealing its falseness.

With a last glance at the bed she tiptoed to the window. It squeaked protestingly as she raised the glass frame higher. She stopped, listening intently as her pulse throbbed in her throat. Deciding no one had heard, she pushed out the corner of the screen she had worked free. At almost the same moment she heard quiet footsteps muffled by the carpet outside in the corridor.

There was only one reason anyone would be moving about at this hour, and it was to check on her. There wasn't time to slip out through the window. The opening was small and she might get caught on the screen wire. And she would never have time to slip under the covers and return the pillows to their proper position before the door opened. She had to hide, and somewhere close.

The cool breeze blowing through the window billowed the drape beside her. Instantly Samantha stepped behind the hanging material, lightly gripping the edges so the breeze wouldn't accidentally reveal her. She had barely slipped behind them when the door opened. The light from the hallway streamed over the bed and she held her breath. She guessed it was Jonas. If he walked to the bed, he would discover her ruse, and she would never be able to escape then.

For long seconds there was no sound, only the patch of light shining into the room to indicate that he had not left. Finally, when she was a quivering mass of nerves, the door closed. Her legs threatened to cllapse with relief, but she didn't move from her hiding place, not for another ten minutes.

With extreme caution, she crawled through the triangular opening in the screen. Every accidental sound she made, no matter how tiny, sent a chill down her spine. Quickly she crossed the narrow clearing into the trees, her nerves leaping at the whisper of leaves against her jeans. She paused there, her breathing shallow as she got her bearings and rechecked to be certain there was no movement from the house. All was silent. No alarm had been raised yet.

She started out slowly toward the path to the boathouse. If her luck held, she wouldn't run into Tom. She crept along through the thick stand of trees, her progress guided more by the sense of feel than sight. The moon was bright overhead, but its light couldn't penetrate the umbrella of leaves.

Danger seemed to lurk in every shadow. The winging of a night bird could send her pulse rocketing. Samantha stumbled onto the path, unaware she was so close until she stepped onto it. She halted, instantly scanning the tunnellike path in both directions. There was no sign of Tom.

Deciding that she could move faster if she stayed on the path, she clung to the shadowed side, moving quickly and quietly toward the boathouse. Twice her overactive imagination made her think someone was following her. Both times she stopped, listening, trying to distinguish any man-made sounds in the night's stirrings. Neither time could she hear anything to cause alarm.

The white glow of moonlight glassed the smooth surface of the cove. A smile of elation curved her mouth at the sight of her goal, but she wiped it away with the sobering reminder that she still had not reached the dinghy. Tom could be there. Using the trunk of a tree as a shield, she studied the boathouse, dock and surrounding rocky land for a sign of him. There was nothing that even resembled his burly shape.

With the aid of the moonlight, Samantha scampered quickly over the last remaining stretch of rocky path, hurrying to the concealing shadows of the boathouse. Leaning against the door, she cast one last glance around before opening the door and slipping inside.

The cavernous blackness enveloped her. She couldn't even see her hand, let alone the dinghy. There was no choice. She would have to turn on the light and risk it being seen. She felt along the wall until she found the light switch and turned it on. The brilliance of the solitary bulb blinded her. For several seconds, she could see only the glaring spots in front of her eyes.

Finally they adjusted to the light. The sleek sailboat dominated the interior of the boathouse, its mast towering toward the roof. But it wasn't the sailboat she was seeking. Then her gaze found the small dinghy, dwarfed by its larger companion.

Success was within her grasp and she started toward it. It was tied near a ladder. Her foot was on the first rung when the door opened. Paralyzed, Samantha stared at Jonas. He returned her horror-stricken look lazily.

"You'll never make it," his low voice said.

Frustration set in. To be stopped when she had come so close was unbearable. Knowing it was foolish and without a hope of succeeding, Samantha started down the ladder. She didn't have a foot in the dinghy when her arm was caught and held by Jonas. She strained with all her weight against his grip, tipping her head back to gaze at him pleadingly.

"Let me go, Jonas," she begged shamelessly. "Please. The others don't have to know you could have stopped me. Please, just let me go!"

His answer was to smile at her grimly and increase the pull on her arm to draw her up the ladder. "It's no use, Sam. Come on."

A second longer she resisted before admitting defeat and let him help her up the ladder. Standing once more on the wood floor, she shoved her hands in her pockets and lowered her chin, seal brown hair falling silkily across her cheeks. Jonas made no attempt to usher her from the boathouse.

"It isn't the end of the world, Sam." There was an undertone of amusement in his low-pitched voice.

"Isn't it?" Samantha flashed in bitter defiance, the husky quality in her voice deepening.

"No, it isn't."

Her lips compressed into a tight line. "How did you know I was here?"

"I followed you."

"You followed me?" Samantha repeated incredulously. True, she had had the sensation a couple of times that someone was behind her, but she had been positive it was her imagination. Her gaze slid to his moccasined feet. "I thought I heard someone, but...."

"I've done a lot of hunting in my time," Jonas replied as if an explanation was really necessary.

"You couldn't have known I was gone," she protested.

"Couldn't I?" he mocked, an eyebrow quirking into his dark hair.

"You came to my room—" she began.

"—and saw the lumpy shape beneath the covers and knew it couldn't possibly be yours." He finished the sentence his own way, glinting charcoal eyes raking her slenderly curved figure with an easy familiarity that warmed her cheeks.

Samantha tried to disguise her reaction with another quick question. "Then why didn't you come to investigate?"

"If I had, I would have found you hiding behind the drapes." The carved lines at the corners of his mouth deepened.

"How did you know I was there?" she breathed in astonishment.

"The breeze was blowing one drape, but the other

was amazingly motionless." Then he added with a knowing gleam, "As if someone was holding it still."

"If you knew I was there, why didn't you just stop me then?" Samantha demanded angrily. "Why did you let me get all this way? Do you enjoy tormenting me?"

Her bitterly accusing tone wiped the vague traces of amusement from his rough features. "I had to know where you were going and what means you were planning to use to leave the island," Jonas replied.

"I could have just been going for a walk," she pointed out airily.

"But you weren't, were you?" he countered. "You were going to try to row across the river in that dinghy, weren't you?"

'So what if I was?" she challenged with a toss of her head.

"Do you realize how small that is?" he asked with a hint of impatience.

"What difference does that make? The river is calm. There aren't any waves that could swamp the boat," she declared, the faint haughtiness still in her tone.

"But there are lake freighters in the ship channel. That little dinghy would be nearly impossible for them to spot, especially without running navigation lights. One of those ships could have run you down without even knowing it," Jonas responded grimly.

"That doesn't frighten me." Denying the shiver that raced over her flesh, she added, "I'd rather risk that than stay here." Her gaze was downcast, but she heard the angry breath he expelled. For a minute, she thought he was going to take her by the shoulders and try to shake some sense in her, but he didn't.

"You don't know what you're saying," Jonas finally ground out with leashed violence.

Samantha acknowledged the warning signal and changed the subject, her gaze sliding to the dinghy. "What are you going to do now?" she asked.

"About you? Nothing. Take you back to the house and put you to bed." He made it sound as if she were a runaway child.

"I meant about the boat," she clarified her question stiffly. "Are you going to chop a hole in it and sink it?" She was suggesting the extreme out of spite for his superior attitude.

"Nothing that drastic," Jonas answered dryly. "But now that I know what you were planning, there'll be a padlock on the boathouse and probably one on the dinghy, too. Combination locks," he qualified, "so there won't be any keys for you to steal."

"And you'll probably be the only one who knows the combination, I suppose." The upward sweep of her lashes revealed the mutinous gliter in her eyes.

"More than likely," he agreed smoothly, a faint glimmer of laughter in the dark silver gaze. "What are you going to do now? Slip into my bedroom some night to see if I talk in my sleep?"

"I doubt that you even sleep," Samantha retorted, irritated by the small tremor that quaked through her at the idea of being alone in a bedroom with him.

"Not very soundly," Jonas admitted, then tilted his head to one side. "What are you going to do?"

"Well, I'm not going to sneak into your bedroom!" she declared vehemently, mostly because it was such a heady thought that she had trouble forgetting it.

"I was referring to any more harebrained schemes you might have running through that mind of yours about leaving the island."

"I'm going to keep trying, if that's what you're asking," Samantha flashed.

# CHAPTER EIGHT

THERE WAS an impatient sigh. "Sam, I...." Jonas seemed about to say something, then changed his mind. "You have to stay here."

"Do you expect me to just accept that?" she demanded in disbelief. "Am I supposed to stay here willingly until you say I can leave? *If* you say I can leave?"

"You'll be safe here," he said firmly.

"Safe!" His incredible statement prompted movement. She stepped past him. "How can you say that? How can you expect me to believe that?" Her hands waved the air to punctuate her questions. "How am I safe when I'm being kept on this island against my will? When you and Tom are walking around carrying guns? Maybe even Maggie has one strapped to her thigh, I don't know!" She was so intent on her declarations that she missed the narrowing of his gray eyes. "You expect too much!"

"No one is going to hurt you," Jonas stated quietly.

"Is that right?" Samantha inquired with a disbelieving nod of her head. "Can you speak for the others?"

"Yes, I can."

"You'll simply have to forgive me for not believing you. I've listened to too many of your lies," she declared.

"You have no reason to be afraid."

"So you say." Her mouth twisted with mocking skepticism.

"Samantha, you have to trust me." Jonas didn't try to conceal his impatience.

"Trust you?" The throaty laugh she gave bordered on hysteria, her taut nerves snapping after hours of strain. "How can I trust you? I don't even know who you are!"

This time he did grip her shoulders and give her a hard shake that snapped back her head. "Stop it," he commanded tersely. "You're getting yourself all worked up over nothing."

"Nothing!" The frenzied note in her laughing voice earned her another shake that rattled her teeth and effectively silenced her.

"You're letting the situation seem worse than it is," he barked.

"Am I?" Samantha whispered brokenly, gazing into his compelling face. "I wish you could convince me of that."

His head moved to the side in frustration as he breathed in deeply to control his rising temper. There was an enigmatic hardness in the dark smoke of his gaze when he turned it back to her face. He studied the confused and troubled light in her eyes, a glimmer of apprehension in their brownness that he hadn't been able to abolish. The line of his mouth thinned as he gathered her stiff body in his arms.

"Trust me, Sam," Jonas muttered against her hair. "I swear I won't let anyone harm you."

"I can't trust you," she protested, swallowing back a sob of longing and pushing her hands against the granite wall of his chest.

He held her easily, overcoming her half-hearted struggles as she rigidly resisted his embrace and its offer of comfort. The fine silk of her dark hair was caught in the shadowy stubble on his cheek. The rough caress was unnerving.

"And I can't let you leave the island," he responded thickly.

"I wont' stay," Samantha declared into the smooth material of his windbreaker. "I'll swim if I have to!"

"And probably drown," Jonas concluded sharply. "You're a good swimmer, but both of us know you aren't that good. And I can't believe you'd prefer killing yourself to staying here with me."

She could have told him that under any other circumstances she would have gladly stayed on any island with him. But she simply couldn't forget the fact she was being held prisoner.

"I won't stay," she repeated, straining against the iron circle that held her fast.

"I'll make sure nothing happens to you. You'll have to trust me, darling." The endearment was spoken very casually as if he had called her that hundreds of times.

But it was the catalytic agent that combined with

the firm contact of his muscled length and her unde-
niable attraction to him that banished her resistance
to his embrace. Samantha relaxed against him, letting her curves mold themselves to the hard contours of his body. She felt the moistness of his
mouth moving in rough kisses against her hair.

"Jonas," she sighed, then caught it back. "That
isn't your real name, is it?"

"No," he admitted indifferently. "But it doesn't
matter."

"Yes it does," Samantha protested, because it
meant that he didn't trust her. Yet he expected her to
trust him when she didn't even know who he was.

His large hands moved up to cup the sides of her
neck below her ears, fingers twining into her hair as
he tipped her head back to meet the smoldering fire of
his gray eyes.

"Nothing matters except this." His mouth brushed
over her eyelid, her lashes fluttering against his lips.
"And this." He shifted to her cheek and the tiny hollow where her dimple formed. "And this," he murmured against the corner of her lips.

And he kissed her until she was convinced. The
masterful pressure of his mouth blocked out all her
fears. Her arms wrapped themselves around his neck
to cling to him, breathing erratically when he began
exploring the sensitive cord along her neck.

"I want to trust you," she whispered achingly.

Jonas lifted his head to gaze into her hungry eyes.
"Then trust me," he stated quietly. "You won't be
sorry, I promise. I won't let anything happen to you."

There was a barely perceptible movement of her head in acceptance of his words. His mouth closed possessively over hers, burning his ownership deep into her heart. Samantha knew he was wrong. Something had already happened to her. She had fallen in love with him—her stranger, her kidnapper—and there wasn't any way she could reverse the course of her emotions.

His hands slid down her spine to mold her hips against him, the muscular column of his legs scorching her flesh on contact. She melted in his crushing embrace, glorying in the golden tide of surrender sweeping through her, uncaring for the hard thrust of gun metal biting into her shoulder and chest.

The growth of beard scraped at her cheek as he searched out each sensitive area along the curve of her neck and the pulsing hollow of her throat. But the rasp of his beard was exquisite pain, heightening her nerve ends to their full peak of awareness. His large hands moved over every inch of her ribs, waist and hips, arching her more fully against him while they continued to explore the pliant curves of her body.

The musky scent of his maleness filled her senses, sending them spinning with delight. Samantha was no match for his passionate onslaught, so she started a backfire of her own. As she sought the devastating pressure of his mouth, liquid wildfire raced through her veins.

After torturous seconds, he let her lips find his mouth, his kiss hardening as they opened beneath his touch. Locked in each other's arms, they both felt the yearnings for satisfaction in the other.

Finally it was Jonas who ended it, breaking away to bury his face in the silky thickness of her hair above her ear. Her trembling fingers continued a tentative exploration of his strong jawline. The pounding of his heart kept pace with the rapid tempo of hers, his breathing disturbed and ragged.

"I've tried so hard to keep from loving you," Samantha whispered with a frustrated longing for satisfaction.

"You have?" his muffled voice mocked her gently. "What do you think it's been like for me? Every time you're near me, I want to make love to you."

She drew her head away, needing to see his face. "Do you really mean that?" she asked breathlessly.

He smiled, a wondrous smile that softened the firm line of his mouth and made beautiful, crinkling lines at the corners of his gray eyes. His gaze traveled warmly over her upturned face, taking in the soft glow of her eyes and the parted invitation of her lips.

"If you don't stop looking at me like that, you'll find out just how much I mean that," he told her with lazy humor.

Samantha laughed huskily and rested her head against his chest. A sweet pleasure beyond description filled her heart with joy. She closed her eyes to imprint this moment in her mind, wanting to cherish it forever. Right now, it didn't matter that he hadn't said he loved her. He wanted her, with the same fierce ache with which she wanted him.

"Let's go away, Jonas," she murmured. "Let's get in the sailboat and sail away."

There was a sudden tenseness in the arms that held her. Every muscle seemed to become suddenly alert. With deliberate slowness, his hands moved up to grip her shoulders and move her a few inches from him. The smoke screen was back to conceal his thoughts when she lifted her head to gaze at him. She could only guess what was making him wary and she tried to dispel his caution.

"No one ever has to know that you were keeping me on the island," she told him earnestly. "Please, let's go away, the two of us together."

Her hand lifted to caress the powerful line of his cheek. He caught it before it could reach its objective, crushing her fingers in his hand until she gasped at the pain.

"You're hurting me!" she protested sharply in bewilderment.

A muscle leaped in his jaw and a glimpse of turbulent thunderclouds briefly penetrated the smoke screen of his eyes. He released her hand abruptly and turned away. "We are not leaving this island, Sam," he stated coldly.

Her mouth opened, but for a time nothing could come out. How could he continue to hold her prisoner if he really cared for her as he claimed? Did he care for her? Or did just being with an attractive young woman fill him with lust? Or worse, had he...? The paralyzing hold on her throat eased.

"It was all just a trick, wasn't it?" Samantha

squeezed the accusing words through the painful knot in her throat. "You were playing games again, just the way you've been doing from the beginning."

"It wasn't a game," Jonas answered tautly.

"I don't believe you!" she flashed. "You were just using another tactic to persuade me to stay willingly on this island! It would have made it so much easier if you didn't have to guard me every second, wouldn't it? Well, your scheme didn't work!" She resorted to anger to hold back the scalding tears that burned the backs of her eyes and to keep the sobs of pain lodged in her throat.

"Neither did yours," he snarled.

"Mine?" Samantha breathed in hurt confusion. She couldn't have made it more obvious that she had fallen in love with him.

"Save that innocent look in your brown eyes for someone else." His lip curled in a jeer, his gaze raking her length contemptuously. "I don't buy it. There isn't anything you wouldn't resort to in order to get off this island—you proved that very conclusively a few minutes ago. Did you really think you had me so securely wrapped around your finger that all you had to do was pull the string and I'd take you away? Accusing me of using you is like the pot calling the kettle black."

Samantha gasped softly. He believed she had only been pretending to be in love with him so that he would take her away. Her first instinct was to deny it, but pride insisted that she not completely humble herself when he didn't care for her.

"Desperate situations breed desperate solutions," she mouthed the words that would support his accusation.

"It was hardly an original one," Jonas mocked harshly.

"I'll try to do better in the future," she retorted.

"You may not have a chance. I hope not," he muttered beneath his breath as if thinking aloud, then reached for her arm, saying more clearly, "Come on. You're going back to the house."

"What do you mean I may not have another chance?" Samantha demanded, unable to elude the grip of his hand. She was dragged along beside him toward the door. "Are you going to lock me in my room? Or...." She couldn't voice the other thought.

"I don't think I could trust you alone even behind a locked door. If I lock you in, I'll be in there with you." The ominous glitter of his gaze was turned on her, rife with intimate suggestion. "It might even prove to be entertaining."

"You wouldn't dare!" she breathed in alarm, pulling back against his grip to lag behind him.

Jonas paused at the door, an eyebrow lifting in arrogant amusement. "Wouldn't I?" he mocked, and she paled.

The door burst open and Tom's burly figure was silhoutted against the night. "She's slipped away again," he burst out. Jonas's tall frame blocked her from view. "Maggie looked in a few minutes ago and found pillows stuffed under the covers to make it look like she was still in bed. The window screen was pried loose. There's no way of telling how long she's been gone.''

"You can stop looking," Jonas said curtly, pulling Samantha forward. "I've found her."

Tom swore beneath his breath in relief. "I thought we'd lost her for sure."

"I'm taking her back to the house now. Get a lock for the dinghy and the boathouse door," Jonas ordered. "Then you'd better see what you can do to patch that screen."

"Right away," Tom nodded.

Samantha was pushed through the door's opening as Tom stepped out of the way. It was a long walk to the house, a walk that was made even longer by the grim silence of her captor. Maggie was waiting in the dining room. She shook her head in relief at the sight of Samantha, but Jonas didn't make any explanation as he marched Samantha through the house to her bedroom and shoved her inside.

She stumbled into the room, regained her balance near the rumpled bed, then turned to face him, frightened yet boldly defiant. He stood at the door, a hand resting on the door knob.

"The screen isn't repaired yet, but I wouldn't try to slip away again," he warned. "I'd find you before you could get off the island."

"Go to hell, whatever-your-name-is!" A rush of bravado strangled her voice.

"Thanks to your father, I probably will," he agreed sardonically and shut the door.

Samantha stood uncertainly where she was, wanting to fly in the face of his warning and sneak through the opening of the screen. But she was convinced he would find her and the consequences might be more disastrous the next time.

A tear spilled down her cheek, then a second. She moved blindly to the bed, stretching out on the covers and burying her head in a pillow. She had no idea how long she lay there in a numbed stupor of pain, her cheeks wet with the slow trickle of tears.

From outside, someone started pounding a hammer where her screen window was. Tom, she guessed. It was only after the pounding stopped and his footsteps carried him away from her bedroom that the tears inreased their flow. For the first time since her childhood years, Samantha cried herself to sleep, silently, muffling her sobs in the pillow.

Her head throbbed dully as the sunlight probed at her eyelids. She pulled the covers more tightly over her shoulders and tried to cling to the forgetfulness of sleep. An awareness crept in, aroused first by the bareness of her skin. She didn't remember undressing and frowned as she realized that she was clad in her undergarments and not her pajamas. She stirred slightly and felt a weight on one corner of the bed.

The painful memories of last night began to surface. She felt raw and bruised mentally as she struggled into consciousness. The back of her neck prickled with the sensation that someone was watching her. The uncomfortable feeling wouldn't go away, and she turned her face from the pillow to glance over her shoulder.

The last dregs of sleep fled at the sight of Jonas slouched in a chair, his long legs propped on the edge of the bed. His elbows rested on the arms of the chair, his hands folded together on the flat of his stomach. Behind the lazily lowered lashes, his gray eyes were watching her, taking in her stunned shock and the trepidation that immediately replaced it.

Samantha quickly pulled the covers up to her throat, remembering his threat to lock himself in the room with her and hotly conscious of her scanty attire beneath the blankets. She had trouble breathing naturally.

"How long have you been there?" Her demand was weakly voiced.

"All night," he answered blandly.

"It wasn't necessary," she protested stiffly.

"I thought it was."

"I didn't try to get away."

"No, and you won't get the chance to try anymore," he stated, uncoiling from the chair and subtly stretching his cramped muscles.

"What do you mean?" Samantha eyed him cautiously. Had he decided to keep her locked in the room?

"I mean—" he paused for effect "—that someone is going to be with you at all times. The only place you'll be alone is in the bathroom, and I suggest you go there now and get dressed so I can turn you over to Maggie and get myself some sleep."

From the glint in his eye, Samantha could tell that he expected her to insist he look the other way while she made her dash to the bathroom. Instead, she pulled the covers from the foot of the bed and wrapped them securely around her as she swung her feet to the floor. Shuffling across the floor in the confining mummy wrap, she took fresh clothes from the closet and dresser drawer, then retreated to the bathroom.

Before the day was over, Samantha learned that Jonas had meant exactly what he said. She was never alone, shadowed constantly by one of them.

During the morning and early afternoon, it was Maggie and Tom because Jonas was sleeping. Maggie was quietly friendly in the time Samantha was forced to spend with her, but it was Tom who seemed the most sympathetic to her plight, his gaze faintly apologetic.

Jonas had monopolized her time so much in the past days that this had been her first opportunity to get to know the others. Yet both Maggie and Tom remained slightly aloof from her. She knew it would be useless to try to enlist their aid in escaping. They were as determined as Jonas that she remain on the island.

At eleven that evening, Jonas announced it was time she went to bed. Samantha wanted to protest, but she knew it was a command he would see obeyed even if he had to use physical force to accomplish it. She couldn't conceal her mistrust of his presence when he followed her into the bedroom.

She hesitated inside, unwilling to change into the revealing shorty pajamas and reluctant to incite a situation she couldn't handle. Besides, how could she even get into bed with him watching her? Her position was so vulnerable, especially because she loved him in spite of everything.

"You might as well change into your night clothes." He accurately guessed the reason for her hesitation. "Otherwise Maggie will have to come in and undress you the same as she did last night." At Samantha's sudden pivot in his diretion, he drew his head back in a considering manner, a wicked, knowing glint in his eyes. "You thought I took your clothes off last night, didn't you?" he chuckled.

Her cheeks crimsoned as she hurriedly looked away. "I had no way of knowing who did."

"Well, you can breathe easier—it wasn't me," he turned with a vague burst of impatience. "So hurry up and get into bed."

Self-consciously, Samantha gathered the yellow shorty pajamas in hand and darted into the bathroom, emerging a few minutes later to see Jonas standing at the window. Before she could slide beneath the covers he turned and saw her.

The pajamas covered more than her bathing suit did, but there was something so decidedly intimate about wearing pajamas in front of a man. She made a project of tucking the covers around her, studiously avoiding the frowning look of concentration being directed at her. Her pulse raced when he moved away from the window. But all he did was switch off the overhead light to throw the room into darkness; then he walked back to the window.

For a long time she was afraid to move. Her muscles became cramped from the restricted position. The covers were drawn so tightly around her that she began to suffocate. Finally, she had to move. She turned, trying to find a more comfortable position, but without much success. The repeated shiftings drew an impatient response.

"I hope you aren't going to sleep as restlessly as you did last night," he said. "I'm not in the mood to keep covering you up all night long."

Just when she had begun to lose some of her embarrassment over the fact that it hadn't been Jonas who had undressed her, it returned with a fury of warmth.

"Thanks a lot," she muttered bitterly. "That's just the kind of comment I needed to induce a restful sleep!" Since it would result in the exact opposite.

"Go to sleep, Sam," he muttered back in a savage undertone.

"I'm trying, but it's not easy with you standing there," she retorted.

"Would you rather I crawled in bed with you?" Jonas snapped.

"No!" The denial was quick and more than a little frightened as her body was first cold, then hot at the thought.

"Forget I asked," he sighed. A task easier said than done. "Good night, Sam. And don't worry, I won't disturb you."

"Good night."

Had it been her imagination or had there been a

slight emphasis on his last word—"you"? Samantha couldn't tell, but she thought it was wise not to ask.

Neither spoke again, although it was well into the morning hours before she finally slept. When she wakened near midday, she found Maggie was in the room with her. The woman explained that Jonas had left for his own room shortly after dawn to get some sleep.

The day's pattern started out as a duplicate of the previous day. The change came in the middle of the afternoon when Jonas appeared to relieve Tom. He and Samantha had been playing a game of gin rummy, but when Jonas sat in his chair, Samantha stood up. His presence dominated the room, making it too confining.

"Can we go outside?" she asked nervously, feeling the disturbance caused by his overpowering masculinity.

"For a while," he agreed, rising to move toward the patio doors, sliding them open, and permitting Samantha to lead the way.

She moved restlessly around the patio, unable to appreciate the view of the gently flowing St. Lawrence River and its cluster of islands. Jonas leaned against a rock, letting her prowl while keeping her in sight. She felt there was an invisible leash stretching from her to him and she wanted to break free of it.

Her steps turned unconsciously toward the path to the boathouse. She hesitated a few yards along the worn trail and glanced over her shoulder. Jonas had moved away from the boulder and was ambling after her, but not attempting to catch up. Evidently he wasn't going to forbid her to go to the cove. Maybe he wanted her to see that the boathouse was padlocked.

Samantha turned her back to the path and continued her aimless meandering pace toward the cove. There wasn't any particular reason to go there. She was only going because there wasn't any particular reason not to go.

On a rocky knoll above the cove, the trees gave way to grass and stone. She paused there, her gaze sweeping the clumps of tree-crowned islands against the backdrop of a milk blue sky. A few elongated puffy clouds were drifting overhead.

As Samantha started down from the knoll, she noticed a motor cruiser growing steadily larger in the distance, but her only interest in it was identifying something that was moving in the quiet afternoon. There wasn't any thought that it could offer her aid. Jonas would see to that.

Strolling down to the water's edge, she gazed at the raft anchored in the cove, but there were too many painful memories attached to it. She dug a toe into the pebbles at her feet, the tips of her fingers tucked in the hip pockets of her slacks. She didn't have to turn around to know that Jonas was nearby; she could feel his gaze on her. The invisible leash hadn't been broken, only the tension had been slackened.

Lifting her head, she stared out across the water again. The large cruiser was coming nearer. It would pass very close to the island, but Samantha didn't take

her hands from her pockets to wave at it. To attract
the boat's attention would also attract Jonas's, and
she would gain nothing in the end except his displeasure and possibly a confinement to the house.

Instead of the cruiser steering a course around the
island, she realized with a start that it was heading
toward the cove. As it neared the entrance, the powerful engines were throttled down. Her heart leaped at
the sight, but her feet were rooted to the spot. At any
moment she expected Jonas to come charging down
to drag her away before she was recognized.

The cruiser was in the cove now and there was still
no sound from Jonas. Biting her lip, Samantha
glanced over her shoulder. Jonas was standing in the
break of the trees, slightly in their shadow, watching
the boat purring toward the dock. His gaze slipped to
her.

At this distance, his expression was inscrutable.

*Is this another of his tricks*, Samantha wondered with
bitter pain. The boat must belong to one of his col-
leagues. Why else was he letting it come in? Maybe
he enjoyed tormenting her. Blinking away a brief
welling of tears, she looked back to the cruiser.

The engines were stopped and a dark-suited man
was making the boat fast to the dock. When it was
secure, two more figures emerged from the cabin. Samantha stared at one of them, not believing her eyes.

He was a few inches taller than she was, his physique just beginning to show a losing battle against
weight, dark brown hair salted liberally with gray.
When he turned toward land and she saw his hand-

some square face and clear, discerning brown eyes, she knew she wasn't mistaken.

Joy rose at the sight of Reuben Gentry, her father, only to be checked by the realization of what this meant. She was being rescued, which meant that Jonas would be caught. Her gaze swung to the path's knoll and Jonas. The trees were still concealing him from the view of the boat's party. Their eyes met, hers begging him to run, to get away while he had the chance.

"Sam!" Reuben was calling to her, a strong voice, vital and powerful like the man.

Samantha ripped her gaze from Jonas, forcing a smile, only half-glad to see her father. She freed her feet from their roots and made them carry her toward her father, slowly gaining speed until she was nearly running into his opened arms. Tears blinded her vision as she stopped before him.

"Reuben," she murmured in a chocked whisper.

He tipped his head to one side, his hands settling on her shoulders. "Are you all right, Sam?"

The comforting touch of his hands slid her arms around his waist, muffling her silent sobs in the expensive material of his jacket.

"Yes, I'm all right," she managed to say huskily, but she wasn't. Her arms tightened around him. Very, very softly, she cried, "Daddy!"

He held her for a few more seconds, then began to gently untwine her arms from around his middle. His brown eyes were warm with deep affection as he wiped the tears from her cheeks.

"I haven't had a welcome like that since you were six years old," he teased. Samantha tried to laugh, but it was brittle and harsh. Reuben looked beyond her in the direction of the trail. "Where are the others?"

She glanced at the two dark-suited men, standing quietly, stern-faced, on each side of her father. She saw the bulge of their jackets and paled. Quickly she looked over her shoulder. There was no sign of Jonas. It was wrong to hope he had escaped.

"At...." She didn't want to tell, but she had to. "At the house, I think. There's a path through those trees."

The two men started forward, and Samantha moved to one side as her father started to follow. He stopped and looked at her, an understanding light in his brown eyes.

"Are you coming?" he asked gently.

"No." She couldn't. "I'll wait here—on the boat."

The two men were waiting for him. Reuben Gentry nodded in acknowledgment, then moved to join them. Samantha turned away, wiping the tears from her cheek and determined she wouldn't cry anymore.

# CHAPTER NINE

SAMANTHA STARED into the coffee mug, wishing she could lose herself in the seemingly fathomless void of the dark liquid. A man, probably part of the crew, had brought it to her shortly after she had come aboard the cruiser.

Half of it was gone and the rest had cooled to an unpalatable stage. Still she clung to the mug, needing to hold on to something to keep her sanity while she waited in the cabin.

It had been almost twenty minutes since her father had left for the house. There hadn't been a sound, not a gunshot, nothing, only the lapping of the water against the cruiser's hull. Her nerves were virtually raw and bleeding, not knowing what was happening and not wanting to know, yet imagining.

She had drawn the curtains in the cabin. She didn't want to accidentally see them bringing Jonas in. She caught back the sob of agonizing pain that rose in her throat.

There were footsteps on the dock, hollow and ominous, echoing over the boards. Samantha tensed, following them in her mind as they boarded the boat and approached the cabin door. Refusing to turn around as it opened, she closed her eyes and tried to get a grip on her senses. She didn't want Reuben to see her torment, not right now. She breathed in deeply and blinked at the ceiling.

"Did they...give themselves up?" she inquired tautly.

The door closed. "Not exactly."

At the agonizingly familiar sound of that voice, Samantha swung around. Her fingers lost their grip on the coffee mug and it shattered on the floor, scattering pieces of pottery and spattering brown liquid. Her horror-widened eyes stared at Jonas.

"What have you done with Reuben?" she demanded in alarm.

"He's at the house." His features betrayed only a firm determination. The gray eyes were unreadable. "Would you like to join him?"

"Would I like to join him?" Samantha laughed bitterly. "Have you taken him captive, too? Oh, Jonas, you won't get away with it," she declared with taut pain. "Not Reuben Gentry!"

"My name is Cade Scott."

"Cade Scott?" she repeated in bewilderment. The name was familiar, but she was too emotionally trapped to concentrate on why it was known to her.

"I work for Reuben," he stated blandly. "I handle all the security for him."

"Security?" Samantha felt like a weak echo. It was difficult to assimilate his sudden influx of new information. She took her head. "Then...."

"I know you must have jumped to the conclusion

you were kidnapped, but there wasn't anything I could do about it," the man now identified as Cade Scott continued. "I was following Reuben's instructions. My hands were tied."

"Reuben's?" Then she realized she was doing it again. "But why? Why should my father want me held prisoner on this island? It doesn't make sense!"

"It was for your own protection. It—"

"For my own protection?" Samantha interrupted. "Why should I need protection?"

"Over the last few months, your father has received a series of threatening letters and phone calls. He didn't take them seriously until someone took a shot at him a couple of weeks ago." At Samantha's gasp of fear, he added, "The man missed, but he convinced Reuben, as I had been unable to do, that he wasn't making idle threats."

"What does this have to do with me if he was after Reuben?" she frowned.

"The day I came to the newspaper office, your father had received a phone call from the man that morning. He said he had decided Reuben should live, killing him would be too easy. He would get his revenge on Reuben through you. He knew what town you were in, where you were working and what name you were using," Cade Scott explained. "With that much information, we had to believe he would harm you. I had to move faster than him to get you out of there before he could make good his threat."

"And that's why you brought me here." She felt a shiver of fear dance down her spine.

"The island is isolated, easier to guard. Intruders would be spotted immediately. We decided it was the ideal place to hide you," he stated in the same impersonal tone he had used since he entered the cabin.

Samantha raked her fingers through her hair, flipping it back.

"Why didn't you tell me all this in the beginning? Why was it such a deep dark secret?"

"I told you—it was Reuben's orders. He didn't want to alarm you. Which is why I wasn't able to tell you my real name. Reuben was certain you would make the connection to his security section and become suspicious." He snapped a lighter flame to a cigarette. "I don't think he realized you weren't a little girl anymore and had long ago stopped being afraid of the dark."

"So you went through that whole charade of being Owen Bradley, then Chris Andrews and the mysterious Jonas!" Samantha exclaimed impatiently. "Didn't you think the constant parade of names would make me suspicious? That's not even mentioning your refusal to let me leave the island or speak to anyone else. Which raises another question. Why wouldn't you let me call Reuben?"

"Because we didn't know how the man was getting his information. It was conceivable that it was being relayed to him by someone in your father's organization. I couldn't let you leave a message where you were in case it got in the wrong hands," he returned smoothly.

Her anger was rising. "You could have explained,

somehow," she accused, "instead of letting me think I was a prisoner. That you and Tom and Maggie were holding me—" She broke off to ask sharply, "I presume that Tom and Maggie work in the security department, too?"

"That's right."

"When you realized that I thought I was kidnapped, you should have told me," Samantha protested bitterly.

"I couldn't. You—"

"I know, Reuben had given orders," she flashed. "But you could have explained to him. I was positively terrified, and for nothing!"

"I did try to convince him, but he's like a bulldog. Once he gets his teeth into something, he won't let go. He insisted on sticking with the original plan for you to know nothing of the threats." Cade regarded her steadily. "I believe you overheard the last part of the conversation I had with him about it and misinterpreted it."

Samantha vividly remembered the one he was referring to and Cade's anger when he warned Reuben he would be sorry. "Yes," she nodded crisply. "I thought Reuben was refusing to pay the ransom."

"The original plan should have been scrapped when Reuben discovered he couldn't join us," Cade commented absently, glancing at the wispy trail of smoke rising from the end of his cigarette.

"Was he planning to?" Samantha inquired with vague skepticism.

"Yes, we thought it was best if he was here with

you in case the man changed his mind and made another attempt on his life, but the authorities persuaded him to stay in New York where the man could contact him again."

"In that case, why is he here now?" she demanded.

"The man was arrested in the night. The danger is over." Cade stubbed the cigarette out in the ashtray, the bronze mask firmly in place.

Yet something in his tone made her ask, "How long have you known?"

"Since around five this morning."

Approximately the same time that Maggie had indicated he had relinquished his guard over Samantha and gone to bed. But that wasn't what made her temper ignite.

"And you let practically another day go by letting me believe I was kidnapped. You could have explained all of this to me before Reuben arrived," she accused angrily.

"Yes, I could have," he agreed with the utmost calm, blandly meeting the snapping fire of her gaze. "But I didn't think you would believe me. As you pointed out before, you listened to too many of my lies to listen to anything I said. I knew Reuben was on his way, so I waited for him to support my story. I'm telling you the truth, Sam."

Samantha turned away, pain bursting in her heart at the sound of her name on his lips. She believed him. Everything fitted, all the evidence that she had misinterpreted. Even the initials C.S. turned out to be right.

C.S. for Cade Scott.

She had known who Cade Scott was. She had heard Reuben praising loud and long the man who headed the security division of his various companies. By some quirk of fate she had never met him until he had brought her to this island paradise that her imagination had turned into an island hell. But the initials alone hadn't been sufficient to jog her memory of a man she hadn't met.

"If only I'd known!" she groaned softly.

"I wanted to tell you," Cade said quietly. "I nearly did a couple of times."

"I wish you had," Samantha sighed, remembering the pain she had experienced when she discovered she was falling in love with a stranger who had kidnapped her. The love had tormented her. At least now she didn't have to feel so guilty about loving him. "I wish you had, regardless of what Reuben wanted," she repeated.

"I take orders from your father. He's the boss," Cade reminded her.

The words were a death knell. Cade Scott worked for her father and she was the boss's daughter, an excellent prize for an ambitious man. And the relentless quality about him assured Samantha that he was an ambitious man. He would get where he wanted regardless of whom he used along the way.

"I'll assure him of the thorough job you did protecting me," she declared with a brittle smile. "You did your very best to keep me entertained, even resorting to some drastic methods, but they worked.

And it's only been in the last couple of days that I decided—wrongly—that I'd been kidnapped. You weren't to blame for that. I'm sure Reuben will be very proud of you."

His gaze narrowed, slicing over her face. "Not everything I did was to entertain you, Sam." There was underlining emphasis on the word "everything."

"Of course not." She laughed huskily to hide the quivering of her chin. "It was good fun for both of us."

A brow flicked upward, arrogant and withdrawn. "That's all it was."

Yet she sensed there was a question behind his statement and it hurt. "Yes, that's all it was," she said, but the poignant catch in her voice wasn't convincing.

Cade took a step toward her and Samantha pivoted to face him, on guard against the explosive attraction his presence made her feel. Like quicksilver, his gaze glided over her face, the vulnerable light in her brown eyes, then stopped on her moist lips. Her pulse accelerated.

"You're lying, Sam. It wasn't just fun for either of us," he said, starting forward again.

She retreated, a fragment of the broken coffee mug crunching beneath her foot. "Please, Jonas...." With a broken laugh, Samantha corrected herself. "It's Cade, isn't it? You see, I don't even know what to call you. Please, I need time to think. It's all so confusing. Leave me alone, Cade, please?"

He hesitated, then grimly conceded. "Okay, we'll

do it your way this time." He turned on his heel and walked to the cabin door. "I'll tell Reuben you've decided to wait for him at the boat."

Cade was gone before Samantha could acknowledge his last statement. For several minutes she listened to the sound of his footsteps as he left the boat. Finally she bent to pick up the pieces of the broken mug until tears blinded her vision and she could no longer see them.

By the time Reuben Gentry returned to the boat, Samantha had washed away any trace of tears. She had even managed to find some humor in her escapade, however bitter, when they discussed it. Luckily her father had no intention of remaining on the island, even overnight.

Samantha gladly accompanied him, needing to get away from Cade before she committed herself to something she would regret.

At twenty-two, she had learned not to give in to impulse. She already had too many scars where people couldn't see them. Cade didn't return with them. Reuben claimed Cade had a few ends to tie up and would follow the next day.

Samantha wondered if he was giving her that chance to think.

Reuben didn't seem to expect her to go directly back to the newspaper. Samantha needed a few days to lick her wounds in private and come to some decision about Cade. There was no question that she loved him. The question was what would she do with that love?

FOUR DAYS after her return, the telephone rang. Samantha stared at it. She didn't want to answer it. It was Cade—she knew it as surely as if he was standing in the room. Cowardly, she let it ring, wanting to avoid the inevitable. But it was inevitable and it was better not to postpone it. On the fourteenth ring she answered it, hardly aware she had been counting.

"Sam, this is Cade." His low voice moved through her like a golden flame.

"Hello, Cade, how are you?" She congratulated herself on the calmness of her reply. It wasn't indicative of her racing heart.

"Fine," was the automatic response, but he didn't return the inquiry. "Since Reuben's out of town, I wondered if you were free for dinner this evening."

Samantha breathed in sharply as he stole her excuse. Cade worked for her father and being in charge of security made him cognizant of Reuben's whereabouts.

"Actually—" She was stalling, trying to think of a plausible lie.

"Sam," Cade interrupted in a quietly firm voice, "I want to see you."

Her legs didn't want to support her as her heart skipped several beats. She clutched at the table, fighting the waves of longing. If the sound of his voice could do this to her, what would happen if she saw him again? To be forewarned was to be forearmed—wasn't that what they said? Wouldn't it be better to see him now than to wait for some time when she might be unprepared, hence vulnerable?

"Actually," Samantha continued, "I don't have anything planned for this evening."

"I'll pick you up at seven," he concluded.

"Yes."

After an exchange of goodbyes, Samantha hung up the telephone, her hands shaking, a giddiness in the pit of her stomach. She closed her eyes tightly. She had to get control of herself before tonight.

The thin organdy blouse of apricot and the long cream-colored skirt gave her a sophisticated appearance, but the luminous brown eyes gazing at her reflection were troubled and apprehensive. Her features were strained with the expression of poise.

The doorbell rang and Samantha jumped. This would never do, she scolded herself, and hurried into the living room. Carl, Reuben's houseman, answered the door as she entered the room. Cade's glance slid past the houseman to Samantha. Her steps faltered under the appraising sweep of his gaze, lazy and warmly charcoal gray.

"Ready?" he asked quietly.

His rough features were more rugged and compelling than she remembered, the dark brown of his hair growing thickly away from the slanted forehead, the heavy curve of his nearly black eyebrows, the steady regard of dark smoke eyes above the angular planes of his cheeks, the slight broken bend of his nose, the strong, well-shaped mouth, and that casual air that hid the steel. Samantha felt light-headed.

"Yes, I am." The breathless catch in her voice revealed the way he disturbed her. Normally, she would have invited her date in for a drink, but not this time. "Shall we go?" Her voice was closer to normal.

"I have a cab waiting," Cade agreed.

Samantha walked to the door, glancing at Carl, who held it open for her and smiling into his gentle face. "I have my key," she told him.

His mouth curved slightly, taking her hint. "I won't wait up for you, then. Have a nice evening, Samantha."

As he closed the door, she felt Cade's questioning gaze. "Carl has been with Reuben for years. When I first started dating, he was the one who usually waited up until I was safely home, and always when Reuben was out of town. He's a dear. I don't know what Reuben would do without him." She was willing to discuss anything as long as it didn't directly relate to her and what she was really thinking and feeling at this moment.

"It's good Reuben has Carl, then," he commented as they walked toward the elevators at the end of the hall. "You won't have to worry about who's taking care of Reuben when you aren't here."

"You mean when I spread my wings and leave the nest for good to embark on my career as a journalist," she added with forced brightness.

"Or marry. Or both." His sideways look held her gaze for pulsing seconds.

Before Samantha could recover, the elevator doors were opening and his large hand was applying pressure on the back of her waist to guide her inside. An involuntary thrill of pleasure ran through her at his touch, unnerving her and taking away her ability to speak. Cade didn't seem to expect a reply as he pushed the ground floor button and turned calmly back to her.

Samantha had the sensation of falling. She couldn't tell whether it was caused by the soundless descent of the elevator or the enigmatic look in his eyes as it ran over her face. Either way the pulse in her throat was throbbing madly.

"I haven't told you how beautiful you look tonight." The seductive pitch of his voice was almost too much.

"Thank you," she returned, striving for lightness to keep from sinking completely under his spell. "You're looking very attractive, too." She forced her gaze to break away from the hold of his and let it rush over the dark evening suit he wore. "It's a definite improvement not to have the bulge of a shoulder holster under your jacket."

"When did you guess?" Cade asked thoughtfully. "The night you sneaked back into the house after your walk and we mistook you for an intruder?"

"Yes," Samantha admitted. "I saw you slip the gun inside your windbreaker. After that, I put two and two together and realized it wasn't poor tailoring that made your jackets so bulky."

"That was the beginning, wasn't it? When you started to mistrust me?"

The elevator had stopped at the ground floor, the doors gliding open. Samantha managed a brief "more or less" agreement as they stepped out. Conversation was pushed aside by the sight of the doorman walking quickly forward to open the door for them and the taxi driver standing impatiently on the sidewalk near his car.

No further reference was made by either of them to her enforced stay on the island while they dined at one of the more popular cabaret clubs in New York City. Afterward, the entertainment offered precluded the need for conversation. Yet the undercurrent of awareness flowed constantly between them.

The slightest contact of his hand or any part of him vibrated through Samantha. Each time his gaze slid to her lips, she seemed to stop breathing. Basically, though, Cade kept his distance, not trying to penetrate her defenses except by a subtle look or touch. It was as if he knew he could destroy them any time he wanted to.

Dancing followed the entertainment. Samantha knew that she could not risk the feel of his arms around her and suggested Cade take her home. He didn't object. In the taxi home, he made no attempt to sit close to her as they exchanged polite comments about the entertainment they had seen.

At the apartment building, Cade didn't ask the taxi to wait. When the taxi drove off into the night, Samantha knew the hour of reckoning had arrived and hoped she was up to it. She nodded stiffly to the doorman as Cade escorted her into the building and toward the elevators.

Neither spoke during the ride up to the floor of her father's apartment. The silence added to the tension that had been mounting inside Samantha since Cade's phone call that afternoon.

At the apartment door, she made a weak attempt to dismiss him. "I had a lovely evening, Cade. Thank you."

His mouth quirked mockingly. "You're inviting me in," he stated, and took the key from her hand.

"I . . . I really am tired," she protested nervously.

The key turned in the lock and Cade pushed the door open. Then his hand was between her shoulder blades to gently push her into the mock foyer entrance of the living room.

"You know we have to talk, Sam," he said quietly, and walked past her, moving familiarly toward the bar in the far corner of the living room. She guessed he had been here before with her father.

Since she couldn't afford to relax, Samantha avoided the comfortable chairs and sofa, walking to the far window that overlooked the bustling city, aglitter with lights. Too soon, Cade was beside her, offering a glass of gin and tonic. She accepted it, staring at the cubes of ice rather than meeting his gaze.

"I'm not sure I know exactly what it is we have to talk about," she said defensively.

"About us, of course." Cade lifted his glass to his mouth, blandly meeting her involuntary glance over the rim of his glass. Her heart jumped to her throat as she looked wildly away from the disturbing light of his gray eyes.

# CHAPTER TEN

"WHY OF COURSE?" Samantha questioned with a brittle laugh of fake bewilderment. She took a quick, retreating step away from him, masking it under the pretense of turning from the window's view.

"Before tonight, I had some doubts myself," Cade stated, following her with his eyes.

"Doubts?" she breathed, trying not to sound as interested as she really was.

"Not about the way I felt," he expanded on his statement, "but about you."

"What do you mean?" Her attempt at a bright, unconcerned smile was tremulous, wavering visibly under his inspection of her mouth.

"I wasn't sure if the way you responded to my kisses on the island was because of me or because you were trying to enlist my help in getting off the island."

"And now?" She held her breath, clutching her drink in both hands.

Cade set his glass down. Samantha couldn't make herself move when he walked to her. His hand lifted the luxurious silk of her seal brown hair away from the side of her neck, the roughness of his thumb stroking the throbbing vein that was exposed. He still hadn't answered the question. It didn't matter because his touch made her forget what she had asked.

"Are you afraid of me, Sam?" he inquired.

"Yes." Her breathing was shallow, nearly nonexistent.

"Because of the way I make you feel?" Cade persisted gently.

As if hypnotized into telling the truth by the rhythmic, seductive caress of his hand, Samantha answered yes. Her gaze was riveted on the glass in her hands.

Her eyes still followed the glass when Cade removed it and set it aside. But she seemed incapable of looking higher than the lapel of his jacket, the dark material contrasting the white of his shirt.

"I thought you were attractive the first time I saw you at the newspaper office, so open and unassuming. I admired you immediately." His voice caressed her, quickening the drumbeat of her pulse beneath his thumb. "One of the first rules a man learns when he's supposed to protect someone is to pay attention to what's going on around him. On the island, I found myself watching you. That amounts to a cardinal sin in my profession, Sam."

"Does it?" she murmured, since he seemed to expect her to say something.

"Looking at you wasn't enough. Every time I got close to you I wanted to kiss you." Samantha noticed the muscles tightening in his neck. "Hell," he muttered, "I wanted to make love to you. I thought it was what you wanted, too, until that night in the boathouse. I decided then that you were using my attraction for you to persuade me to help you escape. But you weren't, were you? You really meant it that night when you said you wanted us to go away together. It wasn't a trick, was it?''

"Cade, please!" She couldn't admit that. Her head moved to the side in protest.

"I realized it wasn't when your father's boat docked. You didn't run to him, not immediately, Sam. No, you looked at me, wanting me to run, to escape before I was caught, even though you believed I'd kidnapped you. You were hoping I'd get away, weren't you?" Cade demanded relentlessly.

"I don't know what I wanted or what I hoped," Samantha denied in a tortured whisper.

"You stubborn little minx! You love me but you won't admit it," he sighed with wry amusement.

"I can't." And by saying that, she admitted she loved him.

His hand slipped around her waist while his fingers curled tighter around her neck. He bent his head closer to hers, and their breaths mingled, warm, moist and intoxicating.

"It's easy, darling. Just repeat after me—I love you." Even word was carefully enunciated and her brown eyes watched the tantalizing nearness of his mouth as it formed the words. "Say it," Cade commanded lowly.

"I—" her lips moved fractionally closer to his "—love—" he moved to meet her halfway "—you."

The possessive fire of his kiss burned the last of her defenses and her lips parted willingly. Samantha wanted only to give herself up to the abandon he was arousing. Desire flamed white-hot, born no longer of just sexual attraction, but now fueled by a deep, abiding love.

She obeyed the molding power of his hands and strained against him, glorying in the exploratory caress of his hands. There was no thought of restraint as he found the secret places to give her pleasure.

His voice, husky and low with passion, murmured near her ear, "It's easy to love you, darling."

Instead of thrilling her, his words had the effect of a cold shower. He spoke the truth, a truth that Samantha had forgotten when she was swept away by her love. It was easy for a man to love Reuben Gentry's daughter. Look at the dowry she would bring with her!

Slowly she began withdrawing her responses from his touch. Cade objected for only a few seconds, then seemed to blame her innocence for the sudden reticence to turn the embrace into something more. He held her loosely in his arms, rubbing his chin against the side of her forehead.

"I left you alone and gave you time to think. Now, Samantha, my love, will you marry me?" It amounted to a command.

"I can't," she replied with hesitation.

His chin moved away from her head in surprise, and she immediately took the opportunity to move out of his arms. Gathering her resolve, she lifted her gaze to meet the piercing gray of his eyes, confused and searching.

"What do you mean—you can't?" Cade frowned. "Haven't I made it clear to you—"

"You've made it very clear," she interrupted briskly. "But I won't—I can't marry you."

"Why? Surely I'm entitled to know," he demanded, trying to control the hardness that was trying to take over his voice.

"Ask me to be your mistress or your lover." She was trembling with the pain breaking her up inside, but she kept her voice steady. "But don't ask me to be your wife, Cade."

"What the hell are you talking about?" Cade exploded. "If I wanted you for my mistress, I would never have asked you to marry me!"

"Then I'm sorry, but the answer is no," Samantha said firmly.

"My god, Sam, you love me!" he argued savagely. "Why won't you marry me?"

She turned away, widening her eyes to hold back the tears. "Don't be deliberately obtuse, Cade," she replied tightly. "I haven't forgotten who I am. I'm Reuben Gentry's daughter. You work for him, he's your boss."

His fingers dug into her elbow, roughly spinning her around. The wintry blast of his gray eyes chilled her to the bone. His hard features were frozen in rigid anger.

"And I'm not good enough for you to marry, is that it?" he snarled. "The boss's daughter can't stoop to marry a lowly employee." She closed her eyes against the contempt, keeping her face expressionless. "Forgive me, Samantha Gentry—" his voice was thick with sarcasm "—for insulting you with my proposal."

The bruising grip on her elbow was removed. A few seconds later, the apartment door slammed and Samantha was alone. What was worse, she had never felt so alone.

REUBEN GENTRY pulled a dinner roll apart and began buttering one of the halves. "Carl tells me you were out with Cade one evening while I was gone." His brown gaze slid to Samantha for confirmation.

"Yes, that's right." It was a struggle to keep her voice calm and indifferent. The mention of his name had the power to crush her, and she carefully avoided glancing up from her plate.

"He's a good man, Sam. They don't come any better," he commented. "I trust him implicitly, but I guess I proved that, didn't I?" He chuckled. "I not only would trust him with *my* life, I trusted him with yours."

"Yes, I guess you did," she agreed tautly, then pushed her plate away, her appetite gone.

"Was there something else you would like, Samantha?" Carl looked pointedly at the food left on her plate, silently chiding her, as he had done in the past few days, for eating so little.

"Some coffee later," Samantha answered.

"I imagine you got to know Cade fairly well while you were on his island," her father commented, not dropping the subjct as Samantha had hoped.

"Fairly well." Then the rest of Reuben's words clicked in her mind. "His island?"

"Yes, it's been in his family for years. His grand-father lost all of the family fortune in the Crash, like a lot of other people. About the only thing he salvaged was the island. I guess it was his grandfather's way of clinging to the dream of what the Scott family once was," Reuben explained in a musing way. "The original house was destroyed by fire twenty years ago. Cade built the present house himself, literally."

"I didn't know," she murmured.

"Of course, working for me, Cade doesn't get to spend as much time there as he'd like." He shrugged. "What did you think of it, Sam?"

"It was beautiful." Nearly paradise, she could have added. For a short while, it nearly had been. She discovered it was going to be painful imagining Cade returning to that island. She didn't want to think about him against that backdrop where there were so many memories.

"Will you be seeing Cade again?"

Unwillingly, Samantha met the sharp probe of her father's eyes and quickly let her gaze fall to the white tablecloth. "No," she answered flatly. She could sense another question rising and added quickly. "Do you mind if we don't discuss this, Reuben?" It was a clipped request, virtually impossible to ignore.

"If you say so, Sam," Reuben conceded. There were several minutes of silence before he spoke again. "Harry Lindsey called me today. He wondered when you were planning to come back to the paper."

"I don't know." She gave a shake of her head in irritation.

"Do you want to go back?" he asked quietly with that shrewd perception that was one of his biggest assets in the business world.

Samantha tensed, then sighed. "No." Work, and involvement in something besides her own heartache, would probably be the best medicine, but she didn't want to go back to the small-town newspaper. Her planned career didn't seem very important right now without the man she loved to share it with. Later she might find solace in it, but it seemed a poor second best.

"Sam." Again her father's voice came, quiet and probing. "Are you in love with Cade?"

Her hands closed tightly over the edge of the table and she violently pushed her chair away, rising swiftly. "I told you I didn't want to discuss him," she protested angrily and stalked out of the dining room, hot tears welling in her eyes.

Her teeth were biting into her lip as she stopped in the center of the living room. She widened her eyes, blinking wildly to hold back the tears. A pair of hands settled gently on her shoulders to turn her around.

"Leave me alone!" she demanded tautly.

"All we've got is each other, Sam. And Carl, of course." Reuben smiled. Miniature duplicates of his daughter's dimples appeared near his mouth, coaxing and endearing. "If you can't use my shoulder, whose will you use?"

"I'm a big girl now," she stated flatly.

"Even big girls get hurt. Sometimes I think the pain grows bigger as a person grows up," he said with a touch of wisdom. "Obviously you've fallen in love with Cade Scott."

There was a painful knot in her throat. Samantha swallowed it and nodded. "For all the good it does me."

"You mean he doesn't love you?" Her father bent his head slightly to peer at her face.

Samantha couldn't tell him the truth. How could she possibly explain that she had refused Cade's proposal of marriage because she knew it had been offered as an easy step to a higher rung on the ladder of success? Cade hadn't asked *her* to marry him; he had asked Reuben Gentry's daughter. As much as she loved him, she couldn't marry him under those conditions.

"It's no use, Reuben." She shook her head sadly and chose a way that wouldn't hurt her father. "He despises me." Which was true. His parting words had been filled with contempt.

"Despises you?" Reuben frowned. "I find that hard to believe."

"That's because I'm your daughter and you're prejudiced." She managed a wan smile.

"Well, if he despises you so much, why did he take you out?" he demanded, unconvinced by her statement.

"Because I asked him," Samantha lied.

"I see." He considered the information thoughtfully.

"I'll get over it," she assured him, but not really believing it herself.

"Yes." He gathered her into his arms and held her close, his cheek resting against her head. "You got over your broken engagement four years ago, didn't you?" he reasoned gently. "But you didn't love him, did you?"

Samantha shuddered against her father's chest, balling a fist against her mouth. "No," she whispered tightly. In another second, she knew she would be crying if she stayed where she was. Tears only seemed to make her misery worse. She breathed in deeply and pushed herself out of her father's arms. "You haven't finished your dinner."

"You sound like Carl now," he smiled down, understanding lighting his eyes. "Have coffee with me while I finish?"

Samantha nodded, returning his smile stiffly, and slid a hand under his arm as they returned to the dining room together.

A WEEK SLIPPED BY, then two. An undemanding pattern began to form. Not rising until nearly noon, Samantha would fill the afternoon hours taking long walks to tire her out and allow her to fall into exhausted sleep after spending the evenings with her father when he was in town. Which was nearly every night, as if he knew how vital it was for her not to spend the long night hours alone.

Three times Reuben had entertained business guests at dinner and Samantha had acted as his hostess. Only two people knew her well enough to see the agony she hid so convincingly. They were Reuben and their houseman, Carl Gilbert, and they kept her secret.

A hand lightly touched her shoulder and Samantha rolled onto her back, drawing the bedcovers with her, bleary-eyed from heavy sleep. She managed to focus on the image of her father.

"What is it?" she questioned in a sleep-drugged voice.

"I wondered if you could get up early enough to have lunch with me today," he said in a chiding tone. "You're beginning to act like a pampered little rich girl, sleeping until noon every day."

"I know." But there was forgetfulness in sleep and that was a rare occurrence in her waking hours. There wasn't any need to explain to Reuben. "I'd like to have lunch with you," Samantha agreed with a tired nod.

"Sam," he said, his expression suddenly serious, "would you like me to talk to Cade?"

Instantly she was awake. "No! Reuben, please, don't do that," she begged in alarm.

One corner of his mouth lifted to form a rueful line. "I'm afraid I already have."

"No!" It was a low protest and she pressed her head deeper into the pillow, shutting her eyes. "What happened?" She wasn't sure if she wanted to know.

"I tried to lead up to the subject of you gradually, Sam," he admitted. "I didn't seem like a meddling father, so I called him into my office to discuss something else that's been on the planning board for nearly a year. Before I'd even **got** that out, Cade was telling me what I could do with my plans and my daughter."

"What plans, Reuben?" Samantha breathed warily.

"Our security operations have grown so large over the past few years that I'd decided it should be a separate enterprise. I wanted Cade to head it and offered him an option to buy stock in it," he explained.

"Oh, no!" Samantha moaned, guessing exactly what construction Cade had placed on that.

"His reaction was much more vocal than that," Reuben declared ruefully. "He seemed to think I was trying to buy you a husband by giving him a position of respectability and importance. He said something else, too." He studied her thoughtfully.

"What's that?" She breathed warily.

"Some nonsense about if he wasn't good enough for you to marry before I made him the figurehead of some company, he certainly wouldn't be afterward."

Samantha blanched. "What did you say?"

"I told him that being a snob wasn't among your faults and that the one thing I would never do would be to buy you a husband," Reuben concluded.

"Did he say anything to that?" she asked weakly.

"He gave me a cold look and walked out of the office." He pushed back the sleeve of his jacket to glance at his gold wristwatch. "I have to get to the office. We'll talk about it at lunch. Twelve-thirty?"

"Fine," Samantha nodded.

When Reuben left, Samantha knew she would never go back to sleep and lethargically dragged herself out of bed to dress. Over and over in her mind the hope kept running that maybe she had misjudged Cade. He had refused the advancement in his status outright. But supposing she had, would it ultimately change anything?

Obviously Reuben hadn't convinced him that she wasn't a snob and didn't believe herself too good for him. And after the things she had said, how could she convince him to the contrary?

She wandered restlessly through the apartment. The irony of the situation was beginning to grip her. She had been so afraid some man would marry her because of her father that she had turned away the only man who might really have loved her. It was a bitter fact to accept.

The doorbell rang and Samantha let Carl answer it, presuming it was the dry cleaners with a delivery. It was a shock when she turned from the living-room window and saw Cade walking out of the foyer entrance into the living room. Joy leaped into her heart at the sight of him, tall and vital and, in her eyes, incredibly handsome.

"Cade!" she breathed in recognition, and would have run into his arms if his voice hadn't stopped her.

"Reuben made me a proposition yesterday." The clipped voice was low and harsh. "He nearly convinced me that you weren't connected with it. It doesn't matter because I'm accepting it and you as part of the bargain."

Samantha stared at him, her joy fleeing. The offer of a company of his own had become too much to resist, she realized with a pang.

"I'm afraid you're too late." She lifted her head proudly. "The offer has been withdrawn."

"We'll see about that," Cade responded with ominous calm.

His long strides carried him across the room to Samantha. At the last minute she tried to escape, but she had left it too late. With unbelievable ease, he picked her up and tossed her headfirst over his shoulder. An arm was clamped around her legs to hold her there.

"Put me down!" she raged as he began carrying her from the room. Carl stood by the opened front door, eyebrows raised, amusement edging the corners of his mouth. "Carl, do something!" she beseeched.

"What would you suggest?" the houseman shrugged.

"Call my father!" she shouted as Cade entered the hall and walked toward the elevator. Doubling her fists, she pounded on his back. "Put me down this minute!" The elevator doors opened and he carried her in, not acknowledging her order. "I don't want to marry you!" she snapped.

"That's too bad, because you're going to marry me," Cade snapped back.

The elevator stopped at the third floor and a middle-aged woman walked in. The silence was deafening. Samantha reddened, embarrassed beyond words.

"Put me down!" she hissed. "You just wait until my father hears about this!" she threatened.

Cade's head turned toward the woman eyeing them with wary curiosity. "Wives," he mocked, "they run to daddy at the first sign of trouble."

The doors opened on the ground floor and Cade walked out with Samantha over his shoulder before she had a chance to explain to the woman that she wasn't his wife.

"How dare you let that woman think we were married!" Her voice was choked by the impotency of her anger.

"It's only a matter of time." He nodded to the doorman as he swept out of the building to a waiting taxi. He more or less tossed Samantha into the back and slid in after her before she could get herself turned around. "The J.F.K. airport," he told the driver.

"No!" Samantha cried angrily, leaning forward to the driver. "This man is kidnapping me. I demand you take me to the nearest police station."

"Sure, lady, sure," the driver nodded, then glanced at Cade and winked.

Samantha turned to Cade, her anger dissolving into tears. "How can you do this?" she demanded.

"We'll be married in Las Vegas, fly back and honeymoon for a couple of days on the island, then come back here," he stated grimly.

"I won't marry you," she denied vehemently.

"You made the conditions, Sam." Flint gray eyes sparked fire.

"I didn't make any conditions," Samantha protested in despair.

"Look." Cade grabbed her arm and pulled her back from the edge of the seat, roughly drawing her to his side. "I'm accepting the charity of your father's proposition. And you're going to fulfill your part of the bargain by marrying me."

"It's not charity." Her brown eyes widened. "Reuben knows the last thing I would want is for him to buy me a husband."

"Really?" he taunted.

"Yes, really. Besides, he doesn't even know you proposed to me before. I let him think you despised me. Reuben was asking you to head the new security organization because he thought you were the man for the job. It had nothing to do with me," she breathed, suddenly hopeful at Cade's frown. "Cade, why do you want to marry me?"

"Answer me this," he commanded arrogantly, ignoring her question. "Why did you refuse to marry me?"

Samantha hesitated, then swallowed her pride. "Everyone who ever mattered has been interested in me because of my father. I knew you were attracted to me, but I thought you were only offering me marriage because I was the boss's daughter. I thought I'd grown used to people using me to get to Reuben until I met you. I love you, Cade," she sighed, "but I couldn't marry you thinking you were just using me to get ahead. Are you, Cade? Are you marrying me now so you can have that advancement?"

"Are you serious?" He shook his head in disbelief, the flint hardness leaving his eyes to change them into a warm gray. "I thought it was the only way I could have you. At first I was angry because your father tried to buy me the respectability that had kept you from saying yes. Then I realized that I loved you too much to care. I wanted you for my wife any way I could get you. And I decided you had to love me, too, in order to go begging to your father."

"I love you the way you are," Samantha whispered.

"And I love you." He pulled her close to his mouth. "I don't give a damn who your father is."

He kissed her long and hard, crushing her in his arms until the power of his love left her boneless. The firm caress of his hands drew her onto his lap as he searched out the sensitive areas of her throat and neck that he had discovered before.

Long, tempestuous minutes passed before Samantha remembered they were in the back of a taxi riding down a busy New York street. The driver's mirror gave him a front-row seat. She resisted the exploring caress of Cade's hands.

He read her mind and laughed softly against her trembling lips. "Darling, there isn't anything that a New York City taxi driver hasn't seen taking place in his cab." But he did bridle some of his desire, although he stil held her on his lap. "A few more hours and we'll be in Vegas. I've waited this long. I can wait until then."